TINA AND DAVID

by
Joan Tate

THOMAS NELSON INCORPORATED
Nashville / Camden / New York

To Teresa Szwajkowska

First U.S. edition

Library of Congress Cataloging in Publication Data

Tate, Joan.
  Tina and David

  SUMMARY: At age ten David and Tina communicated through notes. Meeting again, at age eighteen, they find that writing notes is still the most comfortable form of communication. I. Title.
PZ7.T21125Tr4   [Fic]   73–4382

TINA AND DAVID

I

Once upon a time is an odd way to start a story when you are eighteen years old, but this is a strange story in a way. So once upon a time fits in. Fairy stories usually start that way and if fairy stories are always rather hard to believe, then this is a kind of fairy story too. It is strange to look back now—almost unbelievable—but it started a long time ago, now I come to think of it.

Years ago, we used to live in south London, quite near the river, and I went to primary school there, a huge old primary school with high walls and a large asphalt playground. I can't remember very much about it, and that's not important anyhow. What is important is that it was at that school that I first saw Davie Rawlins. I can remember very clearly the day he came for the first time, I suppose because it was something unusual that happened. One remembers unusual things, while other ordinary things just vanish altogether, or become a kind of familiar blur.

He was in the classroom one morning when we got to school. He was sitting at a desk in the corner up at the front. We all came rushing in as usual, making a lot of noise, and we couldn't help seeing him over there. He was small, smaller than most of us, and very thin. Several of the girls made excuses to go up to the front and take a look at him, and then rushed back to their desks giggling. He was very tidy too, I remember, on that first day as well as afterwards, in a black blazer, grey shorts, a white shirt and a neatly-tied tie. Like a little man. And he wore glasses, those wire-framed glasses which get so squashed and bent and crooked.

5

They were patched with sticking-plaster across the nose, too, and behind his ears. It is strange how you remember small things like that, but I do. His desk was a new one, the table kind, fetched from the caretaker's store to fit him in, and it looked very bright up there in comparison with our old-fashioned ones. He was sitting very still.

Of course, no one spoke to him. I was about ten then, in my last year, and I was one of the tallest girls in the class, so always felt awkward with the boys, most of whom were smaller and rougher and noisier. So I didn't speak to him either. Anyhow, new people coming into a class that has been together for years and years are always a bit strange at first. They feel they don't belong, and I suppose we felt him to be an intruder, coming in so late. But Davie Rawlins was much stranger than most. We found that out on the very first day.

Miss Leach got us all quiet and started reading down the register as she did every morning. When she got to the bottom, she said: 'David Rawlins.'

She looked over at the new boy and smiled at him. He just nodded slightly, without really moving at all.

'Stand up, will you, David,' Miss Leach said, 'and then everyone will know you, as you've only just come.'

Miss Leach was all right as a teacher. She was quite young and she could be very strict too. Of course we grumbled about her, but you're always grumbling about teachers at school. She was a kind person and I can't remember her ever losing her temper with us or hitting anyone, or anything like that. But when she asked David to stand up, you might have thought that she had hit him, the way he behaved.

His face went very red, so red that even we who were

sitting farther back could see his neck going red too. At first it looked as if he wasn't going to do as he was told, and we suddenly went very quiet. Then he did stand up, very slowly, but he kept his head right down, staring at the desk, and none of us could see him properly at all. He seemed to go stiff all over, and I remember feeling sorry for him, because I should have hated to have been made to stand up like that, in front of a lot of people I didn't know, with everyone looking.

'Well, David,' said Miss Leach, and she seemed to notice that something was wrong too, because she put on her kindest, rather silly voice and hurried on. 'Would you like to tell the others where you come from?'

He didn't move. We were all looking at him now, of course, and I could see his hands clenching fiercely down by his sides. He just stood there, not even shaking his head or smiling or opening his mouth. And his face wasn't red any longer. It had turned very white.

'Never mind now, then,' said Miss Leach very quickly, and she too looked down, as if she didn't know what to do either. 'Another time. Get your books out, children, and we'll go on from where we left off yesterday.'

There was a great clatter of desks and slamming of lids and whispering as everyone hurried to do something, anything, to cover up that awful silence from the corner. I have thought about it several times lately, and perhaps we weren't quite so awful as I used to think before. I used to think we were often cruel when we were quite small at school, and certainly there are things I did and said at school I'd much rather forget. But somehow on that day, we all felt ashamed in some way, as if it had been all of us against him, though that wasn't really true. It had all happened so unexpectedly.

So another day started. We were a bit quieter than usual that morning, as if the new boy arriving and his strange actions had jolted us into behaving better than usual. And we took a look at him when we got the chance, and talked about him in break. No one seemed to know anything about him at all, and even the monitors hadn't known he was coming.

'He looks daft to me,' said one of the boys.

'Yeah, daft as a coot,' said another, and they laughed. We all laughed.

So he got the name on the very first day and it stuck from then on, as names you get at school do stick. Daftie David. Or just Daftie. We didn't call him that when the teachers were listening, or there'd have been a row. But out in the school yard, we did. I did too, and when I think about it now, I feel hot and uncomfortable. But at the time it seemed quite ordinary, and I expect I am the only one who knows how much he had hated it.

For the first few weeks, everyone left him alone, so it wasn't too bad for him. We soon found out that he wasn't by any means daft. In fact, it didn't take long for us to find out that he was clever, a lot cleverer than most of us. That didn't help much either. He worked hard and never seemed to find school work difficult, so it wasn't long before he was getting better marks than any of us. Especially in maths. He was one of those people who could do sums in his head like lightning, something I've never been able to do at all. He was always top in arithmetic, and often did extra work, as if he actually liked it.

But he was strange. Even I have to admit that. The

oddest thing was that he hardly ever spoke to anyone at all. He just sat there at the same desk, all through lessons, without saying a thing, sitting very still and staring ahead of him or down at his book. He really did look daft sometimes. None of the teachers could make him speak, not even after he had been there quite a time. Sometimes he would say a word or two in answer to a direct question, or in answer to a sum, but no more. And every time he would go bright red in the face, then turn white again, and he would perhaps stumble over the words, until he looked so miserable that the teachers stopped asking him. We were glad, too, as it always seemed to go silent when he was asked anything, and that made it worse. As if we were waiting to watch his misery.

He could write his answers for the teachers, so that was all right for them, but it wasn't really all right for us. I suppose we weren't very nice to him. I can see that now. But when I think back, I think perhaps we were a bit afraid of him, as you are rather afraid of anything that's different when you're young. He had no friends at all. Not the kind of friends you have at school, whom you tell things to, or discuss things with, or even quarrel with. The girls thought him peculiar and the boys wouldn't have anything to do with him at all, keeping him out of their games and noisy battles. I sometimes used to wonder what it was like to be him, all alone like that. Once I gave him a sweet, just to see what he would say. But he just took it and gave me a funny quick smile and then ran off somewhere behind the bicycle shed. Later on, I saw him standing in a corner of the yard, alone as usual, and he was eating the sweet.

The boys sometimes bullied him. They always had their part of the yard and we had our part. You would have thought there was a high railing between us, keeping us apart, the way we kept to one side or the other. But there wasn't, of course. It just happened like that at school, and I wouldn't have dreamt of going over to the other side in break-time. But once when I was just leaning against the wall, not thinking about anything in particular, I saw Davie up against the other wall, surrounded by boys who were shouting at him.

'Come on, say something!'

'Daftie, Daftie! Haven't yer got a tongue?'

Davie just stood there. I don't know if he was frightened. He might have been, but his face was always quite blank and it was hard to see any expression behind his glasses.

'Sing us a song, Daftie, let's hear you.'

'Come on, Daftie, let's hear it. What about it?'

'Pinch him. See if he squeals.'

And they did, too. Pinch him, and worse, I think. I remember standing there feeling all cold inside. I was scared, and sorry for him, and at the same time I couldn't do anything about it. I was always scared at school and I always did what everybody else did, and one thing girls didn't do and that was go to the rescue of boys their own age on the other side of the yard. Pick up a tiny kid who'd fallen and was yelling the place down, perhaps, but someone your own age, and a boy. You just couldn't.

They must have hurt Davie that day, and that made me feel worse. When we came in after break, he was crying, sitting at his desk with his head down and his hands helplessly stuck in his blazer pockets. I could see he was crying, because although he wasn't making any noise, his shoulders were shaking.

Miss Leach must have heard about it somehow, because she moved him that day. She moved him away from one of the nastier boys who had always sat next to him, and she put him in a desk next to me. I wasn't all that pleased, as a friend of mine got shifted somewhere else as a result, but that was how I got to know him a bit better.

'Be nice to him, Tina,' Miss Leach said to me after school, when Davie had gone and I was collecting up some books for her. 'I'm afraid he's not very happy here.'

'How *can* I be nice to him?' I said. 'He never speaks to anyone. If you speak to him, he never even answers, and anyhow, what can you say?'

'Well,' said Miss Leach. 'Speaking isn't the only way of being nice to someone, is it? You don't have to talk to him *all* the time. In fact, you'll be in trouble from me if you do. But be nice to him anyhow. You usually are nice to people.'

I should have been pleased, I suppose, and I wasn't going to let on that I was usually nice to people because I was too afraid to be anything else. But I was cross at the time, mostly because of my friend being moved.

'She says I'm to be nice to him,' I said to her crossly the next day.

'Why?'

'She says he's not very happy here.'

'But why you?'

'She says I'm usually nice to people.'

'The old beast,' she said. 'Most of us are nice to

people, aren't we? I'm not nasty to him, and it's me she's moved. What are you going to do?'

'I don't know,' I said.

I didn't know. I was ten. You are what you are when you're ten and you don't know much. It is difficult to remember now what I thought, except I know I was annoyed at first, and then I got used to having him sitting there. He seemed to get a little happier, and I'm sure that had nothing to do with me. I expect it was partly because he was in the middle of the room now, and not so noticeable as when he was out there at the front. He still never talked to anyone, but we had got used to that, and didn't expect him to. He used to look over towards my desk sometimes, and once in a while he actually smiled, that same jerky little smile he had given me when I'd given him a sweet. But that was all. He never *said* a word. If he had finished some bit of work and had nothing to do, he would fish a book out of his desk and start reading it. He could read even in the middle of the most deafening noise.

Then I did start to talk to him. But not in the way you would expect.

II

It was one of those awful wet days. It had rained ever since breakfast-time, and so we had been cooped up indoors. I remember hating those days, because of the noise, and the smell, and the boredom of never getting outside. I think everyone hated them.

We were in our own classroom. The hall outside was full of the younger lot, and we older ones were in our own rooms. We were supposed to be reading or doing anything we liked. Some were fixing the nature-table, some were playing games like chess and draughts, but most of us were just sitting talking to friends.

I was sitting on my desk, with my feet up on the chair. Davie was reading, of course, looking like a small gnome with his glasses glued to a book about six inches away from his nose. He was just the same, thin and pale, and neat and tidy. I suddenly had an idea.

I got off the chair and opened my desk. I found a piece of paper and put the lid down.

I wrote: *Have you got anything I could borrow to read?*

I folded the paper up about four times and then put it on top of his book. He didn't move for a moment. Perhaps he thought it was just one more thing done to annoy him. But then he looked up.

I smiled at him and pointed at the paper. He looked down again and then picked up the folded paper, slowly unfolded it and read what I had written. Then he must have read it again, because it can't have taken him that long to read so few words. Then he made a move to open his desk, but suddenly stopped. He took a ballpoint pen out of his top pocket, found a bit of paper, and sat there, writing, with the paper on the open book.

I watched him. There was noise all round us, talking, laughing, even shouting from one corner of the room. The lights were on, and there was an awful mess in the room. But he just sat there, his face screwed up, writing very carefully on a scrap of paper. Then I saw him put a full stop, put his pen down, fold the paper and look up.

He leant across the space between our desks and put the folded paper on the top ledge of my desk. Then he went back to his book as if nothing had happened at all.

I picked it up and opened it.

I have got a book on coins, or a Biggles book, or a story called Children of the New Forest. *Which would you prefer?*

I read it again. I never have read very much, and I certainly hadn't read any of those books. A book on coins? Heavens, whatever was there about coins to fill a whole book? Biggles sounded like a boy's book. I'd plump for the last one.

I tore another piece of paper out of a notebook.

Children of the New Forest, I wrote on it.

I put that on his book too. He opened it just as he had the last one, very carefully, as if it were very important that it should not be torn. Then he smiled very slightly, not at me, but at the note, and folded it up again, put it in his pocket and opened his desk.

The book came across the gap and was left lying on the top ledge. I picked it up and glanced over at him. He was reading again, his head down, one hand leaning against his cheek, so that I could not see his expression.

I never read that book, but that's how it all started. From then onwards I was the only one to 'speak' to him. I wrote notes to him, about all sorts of things. If anyone wanted him to do anything, or wanted something from him, they asked me, not him. And I wrote.

'Tell Davie he's wanted in the nurse's room to have his eyes tested,' Miss Leach might say to me.

Nurse wants you in her room to test your eyes, I would write.

He would read the note, nod at me, get up and wander off towards the door, fingering his glasses.

'Ask Davie if we can borrow his ball.'

Simon and Len want to know if they can borrow your ball.

He would take the ball out of his desk and put it on mine, and I would be the one who had to take it over to Simon.

'Where's the book-list?'

Sue says what have you done with the book-list?

Out would come a piece of paper and that ballpoint pen, and he would sit down and write: *It's in the book-room, behind the files on the table.*

After a while, he always kept a supply of paper in his pocket, and I had never seen him without that ballpoint neatly clipped in his blazer-top pocket. It became a habit. The whole class used to 'talk' to him like this and at the time, I don't think we thought it was terribly strange. Miss Leach didn't mind, in fact she often asked me to ask Davie things. She was pleased that Davie seemed so much happier. Now I come to think about it, it was all rather strange, treating him as if he were deaf and dumb, but when you are that young, you do strange things and they only seem peculiar later on, when you're grown up. We all called him Daftie still but that was just habit. No one meant any harm. But I think everyone respected him much more. The boys stopped bullying him, anyhow, and of course he was clever too, and we all knew that.

Then we were in our last term and exam results came out and we went off to different schools all over the place. Davie got a scholarship somewhere, a money-scholarship, not just passing an exam, and none of us was surprised.

Congratulations, I wrote.

Thanks, he wrote back.

The headmaster announced it and everyone clapped, as we always did when anything like that was announced, and Davie got a prize of some kind too, though he wasn't there to collect it from the school stage.

'Tell Davie I've got his book-prize in my desk,' Miss Leach said to me on the last day of term.

Your prize is in Miss Leach's desk, was the last note I ever wrote to him.

He read it and got up to go over to her desk. Then he went out of the room, and that was the last I saw of him.

My family moved that summer, right across to north London and I went to secondary school there. It was a big upheaval, as we'd always lived in south London, ever since Mother and Dad had married, but Dad had got promotion and this meant moving. Mother didn't mind, but sorting out our belongings and getting my brother off to stay with my aunt, and then the move itself all kept us very busy, in fact so busy that there wasn't even time for our usual summer holiday on the south coast.

I think it is true to say that I never gave Davie Rawlins another thought for years. Sometimes I would remember things about my first school, but not Davie especially. The school I went to in north London was a girls' school, a very large one, and it was a new building, so everything was very different there. I didn't hate it, or like it very much. I spent five years there, and was neither particularly good nor particularly bad at anything. I seemed to have a great knack for melting into a lot of people so that no one noticed me.

I am eighteen now, and I've learnt quite a lot about myself and other people since then. I think back sometimes, and wonder why I was always such a nothing sort of person. Because I don't feel like that now, and I'm not sure why I've changed.

Of course, going to work makes you grow up a lot, but even that's not everything.

III

I realize I haven't said anything much about my family yet. There was quite a row at home, a niggling sort of row, when I first left school and started work. In many ways it was the first time I had ever really thought about my parents as people, instead of just Mother and Dad who were always there, looking after my brother and me.

I didn't know what to do. I didn't want to stay on at school but at the same time I saw that I knew nothing about jobs and careers and all that. My mother had been brought up very strictly. We'd heard a lot about it too. She had been what she called 'in service' when she was a girl, in a big London house, and then she had met my father and got married. She is very good at everything in the house and a very good cook too. So I never had to do anything at home except sometimes help with the washing-up.

So when I was sixteen and said I wanted to leave school, she said at once: 'What are you going to do, then?'

I told her some of the girls had got jobs in one of the factories in the district.

'Not for you, my girl,' she said, at once.

'Why not? What's wrong with a factory? Lots of girls work there.'

'Factories,' she said, shaking her head. 'It's not right for a young girl.'

'But they're nearly all young,' I said. 'And they train you, too. I think.'

I added the last bit, because I wasn't sure either, but that's what they'd told me.

'You think. You think!' said my mother. 'But you
don't know anything. Girls of your age never do.'

And so it went on, for hours sometimes.

Dad was a bit different. I can see now that he knew
how to handle Mother, but at the time I just thought
he was on my side.

'If it's Grant's she's talking about,' he said, 'it's not a
bad-looking place. It's brand new. One of those all-
glass sort of places. I pass it every day. Nice-looking
bunch of kids work there. Ladies, the lot of them.'

Mother banged the dish down on the table and told
us all to come and eat.

'I'll believe that when I see it,' she said. 'And there's
ladies and ladies.'

Dad grinned. He sat down and let Mother dish out
the food for him and then he started eating without
saying anything else. He's funny, Dad. He knows when
to keep his mouth shut, I've realized since. Instead of
going on and on at Mother, as I did, he kept quiet at
the time. And Mother listened to him whenever he
did say anything, whereas she just told me I didn't
know what I was talking about. Which, of course, was
true in a way.

But I found out more, and so did Dad, I think, and
then a woman came to school to talk to us about working
at Grant's. We were all invited to look round the place.

'There you are, Mother,' I told her when I got back.
'You can go and look for yourself. Parents are invited
too.'

I will say for Mother, she is fair. She may be strict
and perhaps we don't always see eye to eye, but she said
she would go and look for herself.

'If I don't like it,' she said, 'then that's the end of it.

I don't like the idea, I have to admit. I'd never be happy thinking of you in one of those places all day long. But I'll go, just to please you.'

We went on a weekday. I was given a day off school. Quite a lot of the girls came, and a small number of parents. They were all mothers, no dads at all. I suppose the fathers were mostly at work, but fathers never seem to have much to do with their girls anyhow. If they are anything like Dad. Of course, if it was a matter of too much nail varnish, or too high heels, or coming in too late, then they always have something to say about it. But my Dad was at work and he couldn't have come, even if he had wanted to.

Dad is a railwayman and he's very proud of it too, but he keeps saying the railways aren't what they used to be. He doesn't want my brother to be a railwayman, which means there must be something in what he says, because his father and grandfather were both railwaymen and there was a time when Bruce wanted to do the same. But Bruce wants to be a radio engineer, so that's one family row we don't have to go through. He's one of those boys who can do anything with bits of wire and electricity, and radios and televisions, and ever since he was about ten or eleven, he's never wanted to do anything else. He's so much younger than me that we don't get on very well together, but I suppose he could be worse.

There were about twenty-five of us altogether, about sixteen or seventeen girls from various schools round about and the rest parents. The factory was very modern indeed, not just new. The whole of the front was glass windows and there were flowers and bushes planted all along the front too. We got there at about eleven o'clock.

'This way, please,' said a smartly-dressed woman, and we all trooped into a large room with comfortable chairs and small tables dotted round the place. Mother sat down as if she did this sort of thing every day of her life, and looked round. She didn't say anything, but I could see that she was surprised at what she saw. So was I. I think she was expecting some huge black building with hundreds of girls huddled over great noisy machines and grim old supervisors saying, 'get on, or else . . .' and now she was sitting in a pleasant room being handed a cup of coffee.

'Well!' she said.

'I told you it was all right,' I said.

'We've not seen anything yet,' said Mother. 'And cups of coffee won't make any difference if the place is not right for you.'

I looked at her as she looked round the room at the others. She was neatly dressed as usual. Everything about her is always neat and tidy. Like the house. She was wearing a hat, but not her best one, and she looked different in some way. They say that Bruce looks like her and I'm like Dad but I never see it. Then I realized that I was looking at her just as someone outside the family might see her, as one of the other girls might see her too. I looked at the others sitting round, and they all seemed to look very like me and my mother. I knew some of the girls, but not all of them, but we didn't know any of the parents.

Mother was summing up everything and everyone. I could see her quick eyes running over people's clothes and figures, and noting those who were wearing hats and those who weren't. She doesn't miss much. I gave up worrying. If she didn't like the place it wouldn't be the end of the world. As long as she didn't take a dislike to everything I chose to do.

Later on we were taken on a conducted tour. The firm made skirts and coats. They are quite famous. Grant's skirts could be found in all the shops and they weren't cheap either. They had a factory in the north of England somewhere and they had just built this new one in London. A year ago. And now they were expanding and wanted more trainee girls.

All this was told to us as we walked round. I wasn't listening all that carefully, as there was lots to see and I'd never been in a factory before. We went everywhere except the office block. We saw the cutting room and the huge sewing room where girls sat at sewing machines. Sewing machines like ordinary ones but bigger, electric, of course, and on large tables.

'Hmm,' said Mother. 'Wouldn't mind one of those myself.'

We saw the finishing rooms, where Mother fingered things, and the packing room, the canteen, the rest rooms, the girls' cloakrooms, the sports and social club, the medical room, where the nurse lectured us up and down like a schoolmistress, and we were even taken round the garage where the firm's vans were kept. One of the drivers talked to Mother, as she knew him, and he winked at me.

'I'll keep an eye on her,' he said. 'She'll be all right.'

The canteen was more like a huge restaurant than a canteen. Along one wall was a modern painting, all squiggles and bright colours, and the tables were all different colours too. There was a stage at one end and a kitchen at the other. Of course you had to help yourself, but there was plenty of room and there was a glass wall there too, looking out on to the back of the grounds where the sports club was. Mother was even more impressed, and I could see her sharp eye looking into the kitchens and at the women in white overalls. I was impressed too, but then I had had no idea at all what it would be like.

When we got back, Mother was very silent while she was getting the tea. But when Dad came in she told him all about it.

' And it's all wonderfully clean,' she kept saying. 'I must give them that. Very clean indeed. I had a special look. I didn't expect it all to be so clean. And the girls looked very nice. Quite nice girls for Christine to be friends with. And the canteen was clean too.'

'Well, you'd hardly expect it to be dirty like an engine-shed when they make clothes there, would you now?' said Dad, his eyebrows shooting up on to his forehead. He always does that when he's pulling Mother's leg.

'Go on with you,' said Mother. 'You know perfectly well what I mean.'

'Things have changed since our day, Mother,' Dad said. 'And if it's clean enough for you, then it ought to be all right for our Tina.'

Bruce grinned at me. For once he didn't say anything, but just grinned. I grinned back. I suddenly wanted to go to Grant's. I'm not sure why. But it had been buzzing with life and so different from anything else I'd ever seen. I was sixteen.

Well, I went to work at Grant's and I did like it. It

was, as Mother had said over and over again until we
were all sick and tired of hearing her say it, so clean.
But it didn't take me long to find out the snags either.
And there were a few. It was hard work. Harder work
than I would ever have imagined, and the long hours
were a fearful drag to start with. But I got used to it.
The girls weren't all quite so nice as they had looked,
either, but I got to know one or two quite well, and
we sat in the canteen together, which after a month
or two didn't seem anything like a grand restaurant
at all.

I found I got on quite well with the work. I did a
training period and earned very little money then, but
at least I learnt the job. Then I was put on a machine
of my own. On skirts. It wasn't difficult work, just
boring sometimes, and I had to drive myself to get on.
But I soon got quick at it, and by the end of my first
year I felt I had been there for years and years.

'And how's my working girl?' Dad used to say when
I got back for tea.

'All right,' I would say.

'Good,' he would say.

'Are you happy there?' Mother would say.

'Yes, of course,' I would answer.

In a way it was true, because I was not unhappy.
Parents ask these things and you answer without really
thinking. I was neither unhappy nor happy. A nothing-
thing to be. Again.

I went to work by bus every morning. A London
Transport bus. It was easy from where we live, as the
bus stop was two minutes from home and the bus
dropped you right outside the factory. At night all I
had to do was to cross the road and wait at the bus stop

on the other side and I was home in twenty minutes.
It could not have been simpler.

And then, after I had been there over a year, my
whole world changed completely. Not in a revolu-
tionary way. I don't mean it turned upside down and
I found another job, or I was promoted to chief supervisor or anything like that. But it changed in quite
another way. I suddenly discovered that Davie Rawlins
worked at Grant's too. Daftie David Rawlins.

IV

It happened like this. There had been a lot of 'flu about and we had one of those sudden huge orders to fill, which always seem to come just when a lot of people are off sick or machines have gone wrong. Both had happened this time. My machine simply died on me. It was whizzing along just as usual, and then there was a kind of whine and it slowly came to a stop. I waved for the supervisor who clucked her tongue and sent for the mechanic, who messed about for hours, but then shook his head.

'Electrics,' he said. 'Need an electrician on this job, it's not in the machine.'

The supervisor looked wildly round. Everything seemed to be going wrong today, and to crown everything there were no juniors about. It was the juniors who fetched and carried, and ran messages. Most of them were girls who had failed the training tests, though there were a few boys who pushed the trolleys loaded with skirts.

I had already wasted about half an hour, and as I was working on piece-rates, I wasn't too pleased either.

'I'll go,' I said. 'Where do I go and what shall I say?'

'Oh, thanks, Tina,' she said. 'I'd go myself if it weren't for the fact that we're short of supervisors too, so I'm rushed off my feet. Just go along to the offices and ask for Mr Kent. Get him to ring through for the electrician, will you? Tell him it's urgent, that the mechanic here says it's an electrician's job.'

I went. I didn't mind. It was rather pleasant to get out of the noisy machine room, and I felt like a kid let out of school as I scuttled along to the front offices. The girl at the desk in reception looked up and said: 'Who do you want?'

She was a bit toffee-nosed about it, I suppose because girls from the machine room weren't usually allowed to wander about the offices, so I was glad I was meant to be there. 'Mr Kent's office.'

She pointed down the corridor.

'Fourth door on the left. Don't forget to knock.'

I didn't answer. Why she should think I wouldn't knock, I don't know, but she annoyed me. I knocked on the door and poked my head inside. Mr Kent was on the phone, and motioned that I should wait outside without actually saying anything, so I went out and waited in the corridor. I had never really been in this part of the building before, so I wandered up the corridor looking into the offices, just out of curiosity.

The offices were nearly all glass. You could see the girls working in the room nearest the corridor, and you could even see right through their offices into the ones beyond, and then through the windows out on to the road on the other side. It was like looking through a telescope, each person getting smaller and smaller, and it was quite funny seeing people talking and not being able to hear what they were saying.

I didn't go very far up, in case Mr Kent came out to find I was miles away. So I stopped and looked into the accounts department, which is only two away from Mr Kent's office. I was gazing rather vaguely in through the window, not paying much attention to anything, and wondering what all the machines in there were like to use. There were ordinary typewriters, of course, but there were adding machines too, and some large box-like machines which I had never seen before. I remembered that they hadn't taken us to this part when we had first come to look round the factory. Too many of us, I suppose.

I glanced right through past the girls, into the second office and saw that there were two men in there, sitting opposite each other. One was a man with a bald head and he was writing busily on some papers in front of him. I thought how like Dad he was and smiled as I tried to imagine Dad sitting in an office like that. He would have hated it. Although he has an inside job now on the railways, it was the travelling about and seeing other people and talking to the other men that he had always liked.

I looked across at the other man. He was wearing those glasses with heavy black frames which a lot of people in offices seem to wear. He was much younger than the bald man, and was leaning over his desk, looking down, both arms resting on the top of it. He was sitting very still, concentrating on whatever he was doing. I wondered who he was. It is strange how you can work in a place like this and never see more than a third of the people who work there too.

Then the younger man put up one hand and rested his cheek against it, turning the back of his head towards where I was standing. Of course he didn't see me at all, but for a moment a flash went through my head and I thought: I've seen someone do that before. Then I thought: stupid, how could you, when you've never even looked into that office before, or even ever been over here.

Then Mr Kent came out of his office and asked me what I wanted. I gave him the message and he made a face and disappeared back into his office again, telling me to wait. I did, and five minutes later he came out again.

'He'll be along as soon as possible,' he said. 'Everything seems to be going wrong today. He's been running round like a scalded cat all day.'

I went back to the machine room, and I must admit I didn't hurry. There wasn't much point as there was nothing I could do when I got there until the electrician came. And there was that odd niggling thought at the back of my mind which at first I couldn't place. What was it? Something I'd seen. Yes, that man in the accounts office, the one with glasses. Man. Yes, I suppose he was a man, but he didn't really look much more than a boy. A thin boy with an old man's face. Where had I seen him before? Why had he seemed so familiar, even if I hadn't seen much of his face? As I opened the door into the machine room, I gave up thinking about it.

Must have been someone I've seen in the canteen, I thought.

By the time the electrician had come and got my machine working again, and by the time I had caught up, which was hours after I should have been home, it had all completely gone out of my head.

'You're late,' Mother said.

'Something went wrong with my machine,' I said, sitting down for a meal.

'Well, your tea's spoilt,' said Mother.

It was rather, but I'd got overtime for most of the extra work, because it hadn't been my fault about the machine. At tea, I sat staring out of the kitchen window for ages, mostly because I was tired and too lazy to move, but also because I was trying to remember something and I couldn't even remember what it was I was trying to remember.

Then I saw him again. Twice in one week. I was unpicking a skirt-length which had gone wrong, the second that day. He came into the machine room and stood over by the door, looking round vaguely, the roof lights glinting on his specs. Then a supervisor went bustling up to him and they stood together looking at the papers he had in his hand.

I leant over and poked the back of the girl sitting in front of me.

She turned round and looked at me.

'Who's that,' I asked. nodding in the direction of the door.

She looked across the machine room. Then she turned round again and shook her head.

'Don't know,' she said. 'Never seen him before. One of the office people, I suppose. What a skeleton.'

Then she turned back and went on working. I stared.

He was tall, much taller than the supervisor and he had to stoop to talk to her in the noise. He was very thin too, a 'skeleton' as the girl in front of me had said. His face looked very small behind those huge spectacles. They threw a shadow right down his face, so you really couldn't see his features at all. Again, I had that strange feeling, like a small niggling stomach ache, that I had seen him before. And yet, I was sure I *hadn't* seen him before. Of course, he didn't see me at all. We were fifty girls or more in the machine room, and I was sitting on the far side from the door, so I could stare as much as I liked without him noticing.

Then he nodded at the supervisor, an elderly

woman, turned to go, and gave her a funny little smile, like a quick nervous twitch, a flash across his face which disappeared as fast as it had appeared. Then I knew at once and I realized how stupid I had been not to have seen it before. It was Davie. Daftie David, and if he had changed a lot in the years since we had last seen each other, his smile hadn't. It all came back to me in about half a second flat. That jerky smile when I had given him a sweet. The same twitch of his face when I had grinned at him about something. Not a smile as most people smile. I sat with the crooked skirt in my lap and stared at the door through which he had vanished. Davie Rawlins. Here! I must have sunk into my thoughts because the girl behind me poked me in the back suddenly and said:

'Hi! Come on, dreamer, the old girl's seen you.'

I jerked back into life and went on unpicking the threads which my machine had sewn so well, but so crookedly, and which took so long to unpick. Davie Rawlins. I hadn't seen him, or even given him as much as half a thought, for how long? Seven, nearly eight years. Davie Rawlins, that small skinny little boy with the battered glasses and bits of sticking-plaster all over them. No wonder I hadn't recognized him. But it is the small things which give people away. He was tall now, and just as thin, and the black-framed glasses changed the shape of his face. But that smile, and the way he had leant his face on his hand in the office, they were exactly the same as when he was ten. I went on working, not concentrating very well, thinking about what I had not thought about for years and years.

It was a little curious. It *was* strange. It is always strange to see someone you have forgotten about. I kept a diary at home. A diary with a key in it, which my mother's sister, Aunt Lil, had given me for Christmas. It was bound in green leather and had gold bits on it, and I used to write something in it most days. Not every day, but most days, and then I locked it up so that my snoopy brother didn't get at it and read it. I always kept the key in my bag. If my brother had read it, he would have teased me, but probably because there was nothing very exciting in it, if the truth were told. *Went to the pictures. Put ten pounds in savings this month. Gave Mother a manicure set for her birthday.* That was the sort of entry most days. Not exactly exciting reading, but of course Bruce would find something funny-funny to say, whatever it was. I think I really kept it locked so that he might think there *was* something interesting in it.

Anyhow, now I did have something interesting to write, and I took it out of my drawer and wrote *Davie Rawlins works at Grant's too* and underlined it. I sat there looking at it for a while, and then I put it away and went to bed. When I had turned the light out, I lay in the dark, thinking. I decided to find out more about him.

Of course I could just go up to him if I saw him again, and tell him who I was. But perhaps he wouldn't remember me, and that would be terrible. What should I do then? How would I get away? Perhaps he had tried to forget all about that school and wouldn't be at all pleased to see someone who reminded him of it. He had only been there for a year, not like me, who had been there for over five years. And it hadn't exactly been a happy year for him, had it?

I'm not very good at talking to boys. Some girls can

just chat away about anything, and are even more lively when it comes to boys. But I've never been able to manage that. I've always been afraid they'll laugh at me if I say anything. So I usually wait until someone says something to me first, or asks me a question, and then it's safe to say something. I get on with the girls all right, but even with them I'm not the one to sparkle. I never can think of jokes and quick answers as some of them can. I wish I could, sometimes, because that's the way girls make friends. I've noticed it. I tried to think which of the girls would be able to tell me about Davie Rawlins, and then I remembered the girl on the bus.

She was often on my bus on the way home. I knew her slightly, because she lives quite near us somewhere. I wasn't sure where, because we didn't know each other at home, but she always got off at the same bus stop as I did and then walked in the other direction. She worked in the offices. Perhaps she'd know. She did book-keeping in the evenings at the commercial school, so perhaps she even worked in the same office. It took me about three or four days to pluck up the courage to ask her, and then at last I did, one evening when she actually sat down next to me.

'Is there someone called David Rawlins working in your office?' I said, as casually as possible. 'A tall man, thin, wears glasses.'

She turned and looked at me in surprise.

'Yes,' she said. 'Why? He works in accounts. Do you know him?'

'No, not really,' I said quickly, because I had suddenly wished I hadn't asked so directly. 'No, I don't really know him, but I saw him the other day and wondered whether it really was him.'

'He's a queer fish,' said the other girl, laughing. 'The girls think he's crazy. He never takes the slightest notice of us. We might be dirt under his feet, or cockroaches to be trodden on, as far as he is concerned.'

'What do you mean?'

'He never speaks to any of us. Never takes any notice of us at all. A nod is all you ever get out of him in the way of thanks or good morning and just ordinary things like that. Snooty, I expect. We're all beneath his notice. The girls have given him up.'

'What does he do?' I asked.

'He's assistant to Mr Grey,' she said. 'He's doing accountancy exams in the evenings somewhere, just like me, only I'm doing book-keeping. Mr Grey says he's clever and doesn't make mistakes, though that's really just a crack at us. He's always on at us about slips that you can't help making sometimes. He expects everyone to be perfect, the old misery. But I don't know if David Rawlins is clever or not. He may be, but he's awful to us. Makes you feel like a beetle he would like to tread on.'

Then she laughed and looked directly at me.

'Mind you,' she said, 'we have a good laugh about him sometimes. But we don't see very much of him. He's a beaver for work and is stuck in that office all day long. He hardly ever goes out of it. Even eats his sandwiches in there. Never goes to the canteen or anything like that. I suppose he thinks he's too grand to mix with all of us.'

'Does he?'

'I don't know, but that's what it seems like. No one knows anything about him. But you'd think he'd at least notice that we were around, wouldn't you? But at

half-past five, he ups, and head down, he leaves the
office, gets into that old rattletrap of his and off he goes.
That's the last we see of him until the next morning,
when he appears punctual as a clock, opens the door,
hangs up his coat, puts his head down and dives into
Mr Grey's office.'

We were getting near our stop, so I began collecting
up my belongings ready to get off, picking up my bag
and tying on the scarf I wore round my head. I felt
heavy inside. I had listened to the girl and said nothing.
It was just like school all over again. I thought about
Davie and all those girls in the office. I should have said
something nice about him, or at least something about
his being clever and shy, or something like that, but I
didn't. Perhaps I would say something to him himself
next time I saw him, to make up for . . . for what?

But how could I speak to him? I couldn't just walk
into his office right past all those girls. I simply
couldn't. I had no business there anyhow, and it would
be difficult to invent anything that sounded anywhere
near true. I'm hopeless at that sort of thing and feel
awkward. The machine-room girls hardly ever go into
the office block anyhow, and it was only because of the
'flu epidemic that I had even caught a glimpse of Davie
in the first place.

In the next few weeks I heard a bit more about David
from some of the other girls who had their lunch in the
canteen. The office girls were a nice bunch in our place,
not like some places where the office staff and the floor
staff sit in different parts of the canteen and never speak
to each other. The girls from our office were always
talking about their bosses. I suppose they always
had before, but now I listened carefully. I didn't ask

anyone directly again, but I picked up remarks here
and there and put them together.

Grant's had taken him on as a junior accountant, I
learnt, and they were paying for his training and paying him at the same time. He had done very well at the
school he'd gone to after we had moved house. They
said at the school that he ought to have gone on to
university, but he hadn't wanted to. He was too shy,
they said, and too peculiar to get on with other
students. Of course I don't know where the girls got all
this information, but it fitted in, so I believed it.

He lived alone. They knew that too, but no one
knew where, except that it was somewhere north of the
Thames. And he had this old car. That was all anyone
knew about him, at least that was all I could find out.
As far as I could make out, he had never spoken to a
single one of the girls since he had come to work here.
I felt mean, listening to all this, because the girls
laughed at him and no one seemed to like him, or even
dislike him, and I felt as if I were agreeing with them,
just listening. But I didn't know what to do, except
write bits and pieces in my diary in the evenings, and
wonder a bit how the girls could have got it all so
wrong. But then they didn't know what I knew.

As I was waiting for the bus one night, shortly after
this time, I thought I saw him. I had missed one bus,
and was standing alone under the tree, waiting for the
next one. It was a fine evening and for once I didn't
have to huddle under the shelter to keep out the rain.
It always seems to rain when you've got to wait for a
bus.

The car wasn't a new one, but it wasn't an 'old rattletrap' either. I was surprised. I'd expected a rusty old

thing with rattling mudguards and scratched paint. But it was a perfectly ordinary Ford Prefect, not very shiny and polished, but not that very old black kind with a wheel on the back. David was leaning forward over the wheel and staring straight ahead of him. I suppose I had seen him or his car every night without realizing it, and had never noticed it before in the streams of cars heading homewards at that time. And of course, one never really looks at cars that go past. Unless one has something to look for.

But he must have seen me. He must have noticed me standing under the tree, although I never saw him even glance in my direction.

V

To this day, I don't really know what made me look in the hole in the tree. In fact, I can't truthfully say that I had ever even noticed the tree itself before. Of course, I knew the tree was there. I stood under it practically every day of my working life. But if someone had asked me to describe it, I should have found it difficult. And I usually stand there in a kind of daze, not really thinking about anything at all, just waiting for the bus to get home.

It was the only tree of its size for miles round. A big knobbly oak tree. I expect it had stood there for years and years before the factories and houses had been built. Most of the other trees round about were much smaller, like the little ones planted round our factory, wispy things which swayed about in the slightest breeze, and like the laburnum and almond trees in people's front gardens. But this tree had escaped somehow. It was on the pavement and the road was very wide anyhow, so I suppose it just got left there. By chance, perhaps, or perhaps someone had suggested that they should leave just one, just one old tree to remind people that here had once been open country. But no doubt that's just fanciful.

Anyhow, I was leaning against the tree one evening, an evening much like any other evening, except that it was fine. I was waiting for the bus. I once tried to work out just how many hours I did spend standing about, waiting for buses. The service is good, but it is amazing how many times a bus is just pulling out when I get to the shelter. This evening, there were other girls standing in the shelter, talking in a weary kind of way, as one does at the end of the day. I had come a bit late, so was at the straggly end of the queue outside the shelter, and I was nearest the tree. So I just leant against it and gazed off into space. I don't seem to be able to think properly about anything until I've got home and had a meal. It was a fine evening, and the sun was streaming very low, straight into my eyes. Even that part of London, which can hardly be called beautiful, looks pleasant when the sun is out, especially in the evening.

Something made me turn my head and look very closely at the bark of the tree. The sun in my eyes, I expect, forcing me to look away if I wanted to keep them open. The bark was very rough and there were deep swirling grooves in it. I had never looked so closely at the bark of a tree like that before, and I found myself watching the small insects crawling in the grooves. I watched one slowly making its way up the tree and wondered where it thought it was going. It was an awfully long way to the top, though perhaps it was just paying a call at the next branch, I thought. The insect disappeared from sight, and another appeared, something like an ant, and it was carrying something about twice its own size. I watched it until it, too, vanished into some crack. Bit like us, I thought vaguely, tiny insects scrabbling about for a living, carrying things about and visiting people. Then another one just like it appeared and I watched it carefully, marvelling at the way it pushed whatever it was carrying ahead of it, uphill too. Then I saw the hole in the tree.

It wasn't a big hole, and I could have stood under that tree every evening for the next ten years and not have noticed it, if it hadn't been for that creepy-crawly. The hole went right into the tree and the bark had parted below it and then gone together again above it, like a knothole in a frame. It was quite round, as if it had been drilled, and the bark had grown round it instead of over it. Just right for a small bird, I thought. Dad has bird-boxes at home in the garden, about four of them. He is always hoping some small birds will come and nest in them, but they hardly ever do. Mother says it's because we keep a cat and the birds won't come near our garden. But Dad is always hopeful; he says they'll come when the trees have grown a bit and it's not so bare.

There was something white just sticking out of the hole. I looked at it, wondering for a brief moment if there were a bird in there, and then I saw it was a bit of paper. I reached up and put my finger in the hole and pulled it out. It was a rolled-up bit of paper, a cylinder about three inches long. I was just going to open it out when . . .

'Tina! Tina! Come on, or you'll get left behind. Come on! Get a move on!'

The bus had come, and not only that, all the others had got on and it was just about to move off again. I hadn't even heard it arrive, I'd been so deep in the adventures of Alfred the ant and his travels. I looked up and saw the conductor's hand go up to the bell. I quickly pushed the bit of paper into my coat pocket and ran, just getting on in time.

'Just made it,' said the conductor. 'Hurry along there, please. No standing on the platform. Move along, please. It's a lovely evening for dreamers. Fares, please. No dreaming about that, now.'

We knew the conductor, and the girls laughed. I felt myself blushing and I sat down, squashed with three other girls on a seat for three. That was nothing unusual, but I was puffed and flustered. I just managed to get my fare out of my purse and I forgot all about the piece of paper.

I remembered at tea-time.

'I think there's some blue-tits in the box on the fence-post,' Dad said.

And as he said it I remembered the hole in the tree and the bit of paper.

'One was in and out three or four times,' Dad went on. 'And I saw the other on the fence. The hen bird, I think. Perhaps they'll come this time.'

'Tibbles will eat them,' said Bruce, almost as if he hoped she would.

'Tibbles is too old and fat to catch a blue-tit,' said Dad. 'If they nest this year, perhaps they'll come back each year.'

Bruce argued and Dad refused to be put down about it. He and Bruce are always arguing about things, and Mother takes no notice. I didn't really listen, but tried to remember which pocket I'd put the paper in, or was it in my bag? As soon as tea was over and cleared away, I went to look. It was in my coat pocket. I took it upstairs to my room. Bruce was doing his homework downstairs and Mother and Dad were both in the garden, Dad inspecting his blue-tits and Mother just looking round, as she often did when she and Dad talked about what they would have in the garden. It was only a small one, but Dad has a railwayman's green fingers, and grows lots of things in it. The only thing he didn't like about it was the smallness of the two trees. He was always urging the trees to grow bigger and faster. I had the place to myself. I sat down on my bed.

I smoothed out the little roll of paper, and I looked at it. On it were two words, written in rather spiky handwriting. I just sat there, looking at them for a long time, feeling rather odd. The two words were *Tina Carter*. My name. Nothing else. Just my name, with a large question mark after it. *Tina Carter?*

It was very quiet. I looked at the paper. Now, who on earth had written my name on a piece of paper and put the paper into that hole in that tree? And why? It could have stayed there for years and years and never have been found. Or anyone could have taken it out. Anyone who had happened to stand under the tree and notice the hole and who had been as inquisitive as I had. I just didn't know what to think at first and, in a very strange way, I was just a little frightened. Heaven knows what I had to be frightened of, but I was; it was quite a shock seeing my name written down like that.

I think I probably knew all the time. I think I must have known from the very moment I saw the piece of paper. But you don't let your mind work like that sometimes. Underneath everything, and with me sitting there on my bed at home, staring at a piece of paper with two words on it, I think I knew it was Davie, and that we were back where we had started, all those years ago, when we were both ten and at school, when I seemed older than him, and he seemed such a shrimp.

Only it was different this time. In those days I had been the one to write the notes, and he the one to answer them. I had written the first note then, but this time he had. And what should I do now? I was eighteen, not ten, and so was he.

I told no one about it at all. No one. I hadn't any special friends, so that wasn't difficult. And I couldn't possibly tell Bruce. If he'd been older I might have told him and asked his advice about what I should do. But he wasn't, so that was that. I did wonder about telling Mother, but I just couldn't pluck up the courage to start. I knew if I told any of the girls, they would laugh. And I couldn't have them laughing at Davie, just as if we were all back at school again. In some ways, they would have been laughing at me too, and no one really likes being laughed at.

I put the scrap of paper in the back of my diary and did nothing about it at all for a few days. I wrote *Found a note from Davie Rawlins in the tree* in my diary, and then locked the diary and hid it in the bottom of my wardrobe instead of in the drawer. Now there really was something in it for Bruce to find out about. I don't know why I thought Bruce was so interested in my diary, because he never came into my room and he had his own friends and wasn't often at home when I wasn't there. I was afraid of making a fool of myself, I suppose.

I couldn't make up my mind what to do, if anything. Then one evening I saw Davie quite definitely glance up at me from the car as he drove past the bus stop, and give me one of those quick smiles of his. It lasted a second and then he was gone, the car just one of a whole line heading for home.

So he knew.

And I knew.

I still said nothing to anyone, but the next day I

slipped a piece of paper into the hole in the tree. On it I had written *Yes. How are you, Davie Rawlins?*

If I have to tell the truth, I must admit I felt a little silly, trying to put a note into a hole in a tree on a busy main road just outside a factory where I worked and knew a lot of people. It wasn't easy to find a moment when no one was looking. I hung about, letting a bus go, and then slipped the paper inside the hole before another crowd of people had had time to collect round the shelter for the next bus. I might have been committing a crime, I felt so shaky about it.

But I did do it. I, Tina Carter, aged eighteen, was writing notes to someone I hadn't seen or heard from for eight years. Writing notes and putting them in a hiding-place for him to find them. Laugh if you like.

VI

That's how it all started. This is really the craziest part
of the whole story, and I wouldn't blame anyone for
not believing me, because sometimes I could hardly
believe it myself. For two months, all through that
June and July, we wrote notes to each other. Two
grown people, working in the same building and living
in the same part of London, and during all that time,
we never spoke to each other once. Not once. So it's not
surprising I never told anyone. I said nothing at home
at all, in case Bruce got to hear about it. If he had, I
would never have heard the end of it. Mother was more
difficult. She began to fuss about my not going out in
the evenings at all, and that kind of thing.

'You should be out and about more,' she said. 'A girl
of your age. What are you always up to up there in your
room?'

'Oh, nothing much.'

'You can't do nothing much *every* evening,' she said.
'Why don't you go out with your friends more. It's bad
for you to be shut up there all the time like that.'

'I haven't any special friends.'

'Well, you should have, that's all I can say. They
looked a nice lot of girls. Isn't there anyone you'd like
to bring home.'

She went on and on about it, so I made up excuses.

'I'm tired after work,' I said. 'It's hard work, and I
don't feel like doing anything after tea.'

It wasn't even true. I didn't feel tired any longer, not
as I had done at first. In fact, for the first time, I quite
looked forward to going to work. I'd said the wrong

thing, of course, because Mother at once began to fuss that I wasn't eating enough and so on. I almost told her once, but at the last minute stopped myself. It would have spoilt everything if anyone had laughed.

Everything was just as it had been before in many ways, except that instead of being in the same room every day, as we had been at school, we hardly ever saw each other at all. It was almost as if Davie had no one else in the world, just as he had had no one else in school but me. But it was different now, and I couldn't pretend anything else. Before, I had just written notes to him because it had been the easiest way for everyone to get an answer out of him. But I didn't have to now. It wasn't for anyone else at all. It was just me.

After my first note there was another in the tree the very next day.

I thought it was you, but I wasn't sure.

I took the note home and read it in my room, just like the first one. Then I put it at the back of my diary and wrote a reply.

I didn't recognize you either. You've changed.

I never knew when there would be an answer in the tree. Sometimes several days would go by with no note in the hole. Sometimes there would be an answer the next day, or even the same day. I say an answer, but they weren't just questions and answers all the time.

You have changed too, but I knew it was you, and I had to make certain.

I wrote quite a long note in reply to that one, telling him how I'd seen him through the glass walls of the office and how I hadn't remembered who he was until later. I didn't tell him what had made me remember.

Where did you go on to school?

I told him, though there wasn't much to tell about that, but I could tell him how we had moved north of the river and that I'd never seen any of the people we'd been to school with again. He replied at once.

Neither have I. You're the first.

One day the note was very short indeed.

I like that skirt.

The skirt was a new one I'd bought through the factory. I don't know whether he knew that, but it didn't seem possible that he knew much about what actually went on in the factory, as he only dealt with figures and accounts. We could all buy things at cost price from the factory, and I always bought my coats and skirts there. I even bought some for Mother too, which made Dad grumble.

'Not fair,' he said. 'Why don't you make some men's clothes, too? Then we could all get things cheap through you.'

'I'll suggest it at the next meeting of the board of directors,' I said, 'and let you know what they say.'

Dad's eyebrows shot up and Bruce laughed so much at my feeble joke that he nearly fell off his chair and then he choked so that he had to leave the table. I had never seen him laugh at anything I had said before, so Dad and I grinned at each other.

'You getting to be quite a card,' said Dad.

I was surprised about Davie's remark about the skirt, because I hadn't seen him or his car all the week. It wasn't only that, though, which surprised me. It was the first thing he had said about *me* at all—that is the 'me' that is now, here, on the spot, not the 'me' that was at school with him.

Once I had asked him about his home.

Where do you live? Is it nice?

His note was there the next day, but all it said was: *Not far away.*

Nothing else at all, and then several days went by before he wrote another note. I felt I had made a mistake, or that he was offended or something like that, but I couldn't think why. So I tried to keep off personal things for a while. He often asked me personal things but never really answered anything I asked about him himself. Sometimes, now I come to think about it, the notes were terribly dull and ordinary, and anyone who had found out and laughed at us would have been justified.

My car is at the garage, being mended. I walked to work today.

That was why I hadn't seen him. If he ever told me anything, it was always in a roundabout way. I asked him how long it took him to walk.

Nearly an hour. It means getting up early, but it's all right in this weather.

I told him I always went on the bus. I got an answer at once.

I know. I see you every day.

Did he now? I certainly didn't see him every day.

What's wrong with the car?

I got a sharp answer to that.

I don't know. Can't start it. That's why it's in the garage. I've been counting the trees all the way to work. And looking at them.

Sometimes I did wonder if he were a little odd in the head. What on earth was the point of counting trees, I thought? Then I asked him.

Why do you count the trees?

Something to do as I walk. I look at them too. There isn't one all the way that is anywhere near as big as our tree.

I had never written *our* tree. And yet I felt just the same about it, as if the tree were our very own property. Every time I saw it I felt happier, even if there wasn't a note there. It became so familiar that I wondered how on earth I had never noticed it there before; its huge gnarled roots creeping up out of the ground, the slight hump in the pavement all round, and its dark green leaves above. They were getting dusty now, and the whole tree threw a dark umbrella of shade round it.

There was nothing remotely romantic about our notes at all. And neither were they about anything in particular. Mostly just ordinary everyday things, safe subjects, the kind of things people talk about on any day of the week at any time. That is, people who talk.

One day he made me quite cross.

Is your hair really that colour, or do you dye it?

My hair is a reddish-coppery colour, and I've always been rather proud of it. It's about my best point, and I haven't got all that many good points to boast about. So I felt annoyed and wrote a snappy reply. That evening there was a note in the tree with one word on it.

Sorry.

I had to laugh. I was sitting on my bed with a piece of paper in my hand on which was written *Sorry*. I smiled, and then I laughed. Then I suddenly pulled myself up. What was I doing, sitting on my bed at home laughing at a piece of paper saying *Sorry*? Just who was peculiar in the head around here? And then I realized that this wasn't really a game at all, as it had seemed to be up till then. Davie was a real person, a person who wrote these notes about nothing much and put them in a hole in our tree. So was I. A real person, not just someone you read about or see on a film.

How would it end, I thought? Could we really go on doing this like a couple of children? Never speaking. You can speak on bits of paper, in a way, but it is slow. And who else asked a question one day and got an answer the next? Who else took a week to say what any ordinary person would say in the time it took to drop a spoonful of sugar into a cup of tea? Although I was quite happy going on as things had gone so far, sometimes I worried a bit.

Once I wrote: *Do you ever speak to anyone?*

It was the first time I had ever even brought up the subject. It had never been mentioned before, all those years ago at school, and certainly not recently. I had to wait days for an answer and I began to wonder if I had wrecked everything. I felt in the tree every day and when there was nothing there I used to feel that the day had quite suddenly gone much darker and colder. I began to dread looking. I had come to regard the notes as my way of speaking too, and I could talk perfectly well, couldn't I? Then he wrote at last.

I can write things I can't say.

So could I, of course. But I didn't. I mean I just wrote things that I would have said if I had been talking to someone. The notes began to get a bit longer. He would sometimes describe things he had seen, taking a whole page to tell me about a bird flying in a park. Or an aeroplane. He was always comparing aeroplanes with birds, and wished someone would invent a silent aeroplane. Once he described a film he had seen, telling me the whole story. He could write very concisely and tell things in a way that made them come alive.

You should go and see it he wrote about the film, at the bottom of the page. In small writing.

Should I? I thought. I would have liked to have gone with him to a film. Then we could both have talked about it. Written about it. It would have given us a lot to write about.

Well, I thought to myself as I tucked that note away, if I want to see a film with Davie Rawlins I'll have to ask him myself. He'll never ask me.

I didn't in fact ask him if he'd come to a film with me, but what I did do was to ask him if he'd give me a lift home one day. For some reason neither of us had thought about that, and it was an obvious thing as he went back by car and I went on the bus. I expect he hadn't dared suggest it, and neither had I. Until now. So I asked. I was a little anxious, as perhaps he didn't want anyone at the factory to know he knew me. Or I knew him. But I asked anyhow, and wrote down my address and waited to see what would happen.

Supposing he said no? Supposing he never wrote again because I had asked too much? Supposing the thought of me actually in the car was more than he could stand? There are more supposings than anyone would believe.

There was a note there next day. I read it straight away in the bus. I couldn't wait until I got home and I didn't care who saw. But no one seemed to notice me. Perhaps no one ever did and it was all in my mind that people would laugh.

The number is ALN 79464. A Ford, on the left at the back of the car park. 5.30.

I smiled when I read it. There was no need for him to tell me the number. As if I hadn't seen it often enough! As if I didn't know the wretched number off by heart and hadn't done so for weeks and weeks.

It should have been simple, shouldn't it? Just to go to the car park instead of the bus stop and say here I am, Tina Carter, the girl you've been writing to for weeks. But it wasn't. For some crazy reason my knees were shaking and I kept swallowing over and over again.

When I got to the car, Davie was already sitting in it, and as soon as he saw me, he leant across the passenger seat and opened the door. I got in and shut the door. My stomach was churning about as it always does when I'm nervous and I couldn't have said anything at that moment, even if someone had paid me a million pounds to do so. So we were both silent. Davie looked at me quickly and then gave that funny twitch of a smile of his. Then he started fumbling with the starter and pressing knobs and changing gear and all that fuss, and we were off.

He drove me all the way home and dropped me outside our house. He must have found out exactly where it was, because I didn't have to say anything all the way, and he took the shortest route. I got out and smiled at him and then closed the car door. I waved as he drove off and I saw him lift his arm and wave back. I went inside.

Mother was in the kitchen. She looked up in surprise.

'Well, you *are* early. What's happened? Got the sack or something?'

'I got a lift home,' I said.

'Who from?' said Bruce at once. He was already sitting at the table, shovelling food into his mouth as if he hadn't had a square meal for a month.

'No one you know, nosy,' I said. 'Someone from work.'

'The Managing Director, I suppose,' said Dad, his eyebrows wiggling up and down at a great rate.

'Yes,' I said.

That silenced the lot of them. Even Bruce.

So we left the tree. Our tree, as we always called it. We never mentioned it at all, but from that day onwards Davie took me home every day. We didn't talk. Of course, I'd hoped we could keep it a secret, but you can't keep anything like that a secret at work. Everyone has eyes everywhere, and nothing escapes them. The girls teased me. And so did Bruce. Even Dad did too. Who was he? And just where had I found him? And why didn't he take me out? Was he a taxi-driver or had he just picked me up? Didn't I know how dangerous it was to accept lifts from strange men? He might be a sex-maniac. Or a dirty old man. And so on and so on.

I didn't answer any of them. I just told them at home that they had got it wrong and please would they stop cross-questioning me. Sometimes I think families are awful. They just never leave you alone.

Davie did speak now and again. Of course, everyone knew he *could* talk. He simply had to sometimes. Especially at work. He stuttered a bit, but not so badly as some people do. It was just that he hated having to talk to anyone, most of all to girls. When we met at the car, he would say 'Hullo,' and that was that until we got home, and then he would perhaps say 'See you tomorrow.' Nothing much else. Instead of in the tree, we left notes in the glove-pocket of the car, the locker just in front of the passenger seat. He would leave them there and I would pick them up and put them in my pocket. He didn't fetch me in the mornings, just took me home in the evenings.

Sometimes I would say something, about the weather, or the car, or about work, and he would nod, or shake his head. Sometimes we just wrote notes as before. Davie found it easier to write things down, and now he had found someone to write things *to*. So had I.

VII

Davie always drove the car with a kind of steady concentration. As we didn't talk and as we were always in a stream of home-going traffic, I used to let my mind wander. And my eyes.

Once I saw a motoring magazine lying in the locker just in front of me, and idly I picked it up. There was a label stuck on the back.

> D. L. Rawlins, Esq.,
> Flat A,
> 19 Caton Avenue,
> N.14.

I didn't mean to be nosy, but I couldn't help seeing the address. Caton Avenue! That wasn't more than five or six streets away from where we lived! He lived quite near and had never said anything. I was just going to burst out with it and then I didn't. Carefully I put the magazine back and looked out of the window.

He dropped me and drove on. I went slowly into the house and straight up to my room. I brushed my hair and made a lot of noise in the bathroom, just so that Mother would know I was getting tidied up for tea. I don't know why I went through all that circus, because I usually just washed and sat down to tea at once. But I felt I couldn't face them just yet.

All this time he had lived just round the corner and had said nothing about it. Why? I went down to tea, where they were talking about holidays. We always went to the south coast for a week, and that was what we were going to do again this year. Then we had a week at home. The factory was to close down for those two weeks for the holidays and Dad had got two weeks of his holidays then too.

'You could do with a bit of sun and fresh air, my girl,' said Mother. 'What's up with you?'

'Nothing,' I said. 'Roll on the holidays.'

'Perhaps it'll be our last family holiday,' said Mother, 'so we'd better make the most of it.'

'Why, what's happening next year?' said Bruce, and Dad looked enquiringly at Mother too.

'I didn't mean anything special,' Mother said quickly. 'Just that you're both getting older and perhaps you'll want to do something on your own next year.'

'Some of the girls are going abroad,' I said. 'A whole party of them together, going to France. They asked me if I'd like to go with them. It's not all that expensive.'

'Why didn't you?' said Bruce.

'Perhaps I will next year,' I said. 'I've been thinking about it.'

I hadn't been thinking about it at all, but I'd got into the habit of saying things like that to the family. Anything to keep them off the subject of Davie. That evening I couldn't help thinking about him living so near. I couldn't help feeling a bit hurt. After tea I walked round in the direction of his street and just stood there, at the top of the street, staring down it. Then I went home. If he didn't want me to know, that was that.

I wrote in my diary that night: *Davie lives in Caton Avenue.*

Then I looked back through the entries of the past

months and wondered. Davie's notes made quite a thick pack in the back now. I should have to find somewhere else to keep them or the diary wouldn't lock soon.

I closed the diary and put it away. In bed that night I lay awake and thought about it. *I walked to work this morning.* He must have walked the way I usually went by bus. *I counted the trees.* They must have been the same trees that I saw every day too. *I like that skirt.* Perhaps it was here that he had seen me, in that skirt, not at work? I tried to imagine what was going on in his mind, what he thought. I tried to imagine what Flat A was like. But I just couldn't. I realized then that I knew nothing about Davie at all. Nothing. I think that was the first time the idea came into my head, but as usual, I pushed it down to where it got forgotten. Next morning I looked in the mirror and there was myself, as usual, quite nice reddish-coppery hair, an ordinary face, blue eyes, high cheekbones, me, just as I am most days. I decided I didn't know much about myself either.

But I must have changed a bit. Because on that Sunday afternoon, I put my summer coat round my shoulders and walked round to Caton Avenue again. This time I didn't stand staring foolishly down the street, but went to Number 19 and stood outside the gate. Then I went inside the untidy wild front garden. There was a row of bells with cards stuck against them beside the front door, and a notice saying Flat A with an arrow pointing round the back. I walked along the path and turned the corner of the house. There was the old back door of the house, and on the door, *Flat A.* The back garden was in the same state as the front.

I must have stood there at least three minutes. There

was no bell and no sign of life at all. I knocked. At first it was completely silent and then I heard steps the other side. Davie opened the door.

When he saw me he went quite white and put his hand up to his glasses.

'Hullo,' I said. 'I heard you lived here, so I thought I'd call. I haven't any visiting cards, I'm afraid.'

I could hear that my voice was rather shrill, and the laugh I gave was a silly laugh. Davie made as if to shut the door and then seemed to change his mind. He stepped back and made a gesture for me to come in.

It was a dark shabby little house, and Davie's room must have once been the kitchen. I stepped inside and Davie closed the door behind me. Then he stood there, helplessly. I wished more than anything else that I hadn't come.

It was a bare room, with hardly any furniture in it at all. A bed against one wall, a wooden table and chair against the other. A fireplace and an armchair, one of those old red velvety ones you see in salerooms and second-hand shops. There was a cupboard by the door and a chest-of-drawers, and that was all. On the table lay an open book and a file, and some notebooks, a fountain pen lying neatly along the side of the file. There was a row of books standing tidily at the back of the table, against the wall. The curtains were a dull, yellowish brown colour, and the bedspread of the same material. There was a small rug on the floor, but otherwise the boards were covered with bare brown lino. It was clean, neat, cold and about as friendly as a crocodile's smile.

I picked up the pen and tore a piece of paper off a note-pad that was lying by the file.

Were you working? I'll go if you like.

He shook his head. Then he pointed to the arm-chair and I sat down. He sat down on the chair by the table and for a moment just looked at me. I wished more than ever that I had not come. For a moment I thought he was going to say something, and then he turned away and scribbled on the pad.

You're the first visitor I've ever had.

'Do you live here quite alone?' I said out aloud.

He nodded.

'Don't you know any of the other people who live in the other flats?'

He shook his head. Then he leant over and switched on a small transistor wireless on top of the row of books. I said a little louder, above the music: 'Would you like to come back home for tea?'

I don't know what made me say it, because I'd said nothing at home, but I was desperate.

He went rigid at once, and I remembered him standing at his desk all those years ago, clenching and un-clenching his fists. He was doing the same now. Then he switched off the radio and wrote on the pad, tearing the paper off so roughly that the top edge was all ragged.

Don't ask me.

I sat there for a while and then I couldn't bear it any longer. I got up and went towards the door. I hadn't been there more than ten minutes at the most.

'See you tomorrow,' I said, miserably.

He had hardly moved, and was sitting at the table, his back almost turned towards me. Suddenly I knew that if I stayed a moment longer, he would break. I don't know how I knew, but I did, and some streak of sense somewhere or other in my silly head told me to go and go quickly. I opened the door, slipped out and then closed the door quickly behind me. I walked home, telling myself that I was stupid, that I should never have gone without warning him, that I'd made a fool of myself again, that I'd made things worse, and so on and so on. I wished I understood. I wished I knew what to do.

Next day was just like any other day. Only the car wasn't there, and neither was there a note in the tree. Tuesday was the same. Wednesday the same. On Thursday, the car was there, and at half-past five, I went to the car park, got in the car and we drove home. There was a note in the glove-compartment. I picked it up and put it in my pocket.

I'm no good. But don't leave me.

That's all. No explanation. Nothing about why he had been away three days. I wondered what happened to him when he was ill in that bare room.

Friday came. He was there. There was no note. When I got out of the car, I leant down and said:

'I'll be away a week. See you after that?'

He nodded without smiling, and waved.

I think I must have been very strung up, because when we got to the south coast, I could do nothing but sleep and lie about in the sun. We were lucky with the weather and it was hot all the week. We always stayed with the same person, and she had known us since we were children. Bruce had quite a bunch of 'summer friends' whom he met every year, and the whole gang of them went climbing round the rocks and up the cliffs all day, so I didn't see much of them.

As I lay in the sun I tried to sort things out, and I

began to see that it was hopeless, that I couldn't talk to Davie, and he couldn't talk to me. He needed someone quite different from me, someone cheerful and jolly, someone who would chat easily and slowly get him to talk too. Not someone who was afraid half the time, as I was. I tried to think out what I thought of him, too, and that wasn't easy. Was I fond of him? I couldn't really tell. Was I just playing a game? Sometimes it seemed like that. And yet, as the days went by and I got quite a good tan, especially for a redhead, I found I was missing him. Missing him far more than I would have thought possible. I found that I thought about him more than anything else, but then pulled myself up when I realized that I hadn't anything much else to think about.

Nothing ever turns out as you think it is going to. I think I had always thought that one day I would meet someone whom I'd fall in love with and who would fall in love with me and that would be that. We'd get engaged and there would be a wedding and we would have a home and grumble about the relations, just like everyone else. Now I saw that perhaps things never are as simple as that, for anyone, and they didn't look like being simple at all for me. I knew no one well, and the only person I ever thought about was a strange thin boy of my own age, whom I liked, but not with any great feeling that I couldn't possibly live without him, which I thought you had to think.

Then I thought of that *I'm no good. But don't leave me.* Perhaps he meant it. Perhaps he felt a little that way about me. And perhaps when I felt sorry for him, I wasn't feeling sorry for him at all, but sorry for myself.

'You're looking better, my girl,' said Mother that evening. 'We should stay on another week.'

'No,' I said quickly, 'let's go back now.'

Then I hurriedly added: 'The weather might not hold and we'd regret it.'

Then I knew that I did want to get back. Despite the sun and fresh air, I did not want to stay another week. When I saw the note on the doormat inside the front door when we got in, I felt a sudden lift inside me, and I picked it up. No stamp, so he must have brought it round himself.

VIII

*What about Battersea Fun Fair on Saturday? We could
go by the river. 7.30 by the tree?*

I didn't answer it. It would be a test. I had been to
Battersea years and years ago, when I was small. It
wasn't far from where we used to live and I remembered being taken there and that was about all. It was
bright and noisy. It would be fun to go again. Fun? I
was glad to be back in London.

I had to catch a bus to get to the tree. Of course it
meant going in the wrong direction for Battersea. But
perhaps Davie had been uncertain too, and hadn't
wanted to come to the house. *Don't ask me.* The tree
was a good place to meet, anyhow. To start again.

It was still fine and I put on a summer dress and took
a light jacket with me. I was there at a quarter past
seven and had to wait. I stood by the tree and looked at
it. There were still insects crawling up the bark and I
made myself not look in the hole. For about five
minutes. Then I poked my finger into it and there was
a note in it.

At once I thought that he had changed his mind, that
he couldn't come, that he was ill, anything . . . the
whole day went flat.

Shan't be long.

I smiled and stuffed the bit of paper into my jacket
pocket. He knew I'd look in the hole if I had to wait.
And if I'd been late, he would have been there, so there
would have been no need for a note, so it could rot
away and I would never have known.

He wasn't long. I saw the car coming quite a long

way away, but pretended not to. When it stopped I looked surprised and got in with a smile. There was no one about, as all the factories round there were closed, so I don't know who I was acting like that for. Davie, I suppose, and I'm sure he didn't notice. The whole area seemed strangely quiet. He didn't start the car off straight away, but put his hand into his jacket pocket and pulled out a piece of paper. He didn't give it to me but opened it out flat and then reached across and held it about six inches from my nose.

Nice to see you again.

I laughed out aloud, holding his wrist so that I could read the note. Then Davie snatched his hand away, took a pencil out of his pocket, rested the note against the windscreen and added *Very* in front of the *Nice.*

I took the pencil and wrote *Nice to see you, too.* Anyone looking into the car would have thought we were both quite mad.

Davie took off his glasses and wiped the lenses clean with his handkerchief, put them on and we set off on the long drive to Westminster Pier.

Without his glasses Davie had looked just like a small boy again. His face was very thin and he had small flat ears and rather short hair. It was the first time I'd seen him without a formal grey suit on too. He had a light jacket on and a summer shirt. With his glasses off, his eyes looked quite blank, as if strong light hurt them. He screwed them up tightly and then opened them again before putting his glasses on. I suppose he hid himself behind the glasses, the bigger and blacker the better, just as he hid behind the notes.

We left the car down a side street near the Houses of Parliament and went down to the pier. The river boat was in, so Davie bought two tickets and we managed to get seats right at the front of the boat. It was very crowded. The summer holidays always bring thousands of people to London, while half London goes off somewhere else. One of the things people from outside London seemed to like doing most was taking these trips up and down the river. Dad always said they liked it because it took the weight off their feet. This boat went on up to Kew Gardens, another favourite trip, but we were getting off at Battersea Pier.

It was fun milling round with a lot of people, and it was lovely sitting up in front. We turned and looked the way we were going and the wind blew quite strongly into our faces. Davie put his arm along the rail behind me and we listened to the man telling all the passengers what the buildings on the river banks were. I knew most of them, but then so I should, as I was born and bred in London, and apart from our summer holidays by the sea I had never been anywhere else.

But I didn't know all of them, and there were several buildings which I'd never seen before. The announcer was a bit of a funny man, too, and made jokes all the way, pulling the visitors' legs and telling tall stories which we all knew weren't true.

I turned to say something to Davie, but then kept my mouth shut. This wasn't the place for taking out bits of paper and writing notes, and neither was it a place for questions. There was too much noise, what with the crowds of people, the man bawling through a microphone, the wind in our ears and the engine of the boat. So we just sat there, enjoying the sun and the wind, and I felt content.

We climbed up the ramp and went straight into the

fair. At first, we just walked round and looked at everything, and then we had a go at the stalls, rolling pennies, which we lost, riding in ridiculous paddle boats, sliding down the helter-skelter, and trying several roundabouts. I hadn't done things like that since I was a child.

We stopped at a shooting gallery and Davie had a go. You had to shoot ping-pong balls off spouts of water. He was good at it, too, amazingly skilful when you knew his sight wasn't very good, and he won a large stuffed doll with wobbly googly eyes.

He handed the doll to me and fished out his ball-point pen again. *My lucky day* he wrote on the back of it.

We sat down for a cup of tea fairly late and watched the people walking about, until it got quite dark. By nine o'clock it was really dark and the lights strung between the trees and round the fun fair made the whole place look very gay. The music blared out of the loudspeakers everywhere and children rushed screaming about. There was no need to talk, and even if we had wanted to we would not have been able to hear.

Then we came to the Big Dipper. We stood watching the wagons hurtling up and down for a while, and then Davie turned to me and pointed to the ticket office, raising his eyebrows.

I had never been on a switchback before and I wasn't very sure that I wanted to, either. We had seen it most of the evening, and heard it; the rumble of the wheels and the shrieks and yells of the people in the wagons as they roared down the slopes above us. It had been part of the fun of the place, but now it was actually a question of going on it, I wasn't at all sure.

David got a stick from the ground and then scrawled in the sand under a light: *Been on one before?*

I shook my head. His eyes looked unnaturally bright under the lamp post.

He wrote in the sand again. *Neither have I.*

Then he lifted the stick up and was just about to write something more, when he hesitated, turned to me and said perfectly clearly:

'But let's try, shall we?'

I was taken by surprise. For a moment I couldn't answer.

'Come on,' he said. 'I'm the one who's supposed to be dumb, not you. Do you want to try?'

I nodded and smiled at him. He went across to the booth to get the tickets. While we were waiting to get on, I said: 'I'm not so sure now. I'm not sure I'm going to like it.'

He looked at me and said: 'Would you rather not? We don't have to.'

I hesitated. But he had bought the tickets and there were people behind us. Anyhow, it was time I stopped backing out of everything.

'Oh, let's try,' I said quickly, trying to convince myself that I would enjoy it. 'Try anything once.'

David held my elbow when we got into the wagon and the attendant came to fix the bar across in front of us. I must admit I was quite frightened, and if I hadn't been on the far side, with Davie between me and the way out of the wagon, I should probably have got out before it had started. But I didn't. At first the wagon went slowly, but it soon picked up speed. I hung on very tightly to the brass bar with both hands, and I saw that Davie was doing the same. The wagon got faster and faster and every time we tipped over the top and started rushing down the slope the other side, I could feel all my insides floating along behind me. At least, that's what it seemed like. The crowd below and the trees with the lights hanging in them and the lights from the stalls all became one blinding blur of noise and confusion. Then after the first few times, I must have got used to it, because I began to enjoy it. The wind tore through my hair and I could feel myself gasping like a fish as we set off again downhill. My hair was streaming out behind my head and my eyes were watering so that I could hardly see anything.

Then, right in the middle of one of those terrible downward swoops, I found myself thinking quite clearly, as if I were lying peacefully on a beach somewhere.

We were talking. We were talking just like ordinary people. Davie was talking. And he started it.

'I'm the one who's supposed to be dumb, not you.'

That's what he'd said, hadn't he, or had I dreamt it? I turned my head to look at Davie. He seemed to know exactly what I'd been thinking, because he smiled and shook his head, as if to say, no, you didn't dream it, and then we both laughed out aloud as we swooped up the other side again. Of course we couldn't hear each other laugh, because of the noise, but they were real laughs and it quite changed Davie's face. When I thought about it, up there, whirling about above the treetops on this fine summer evening, I realized I had never seen him laugh before. Not once. Ever.

Then the wagon began to slow down and gradually it let us go. I was tired out. I felt just as if I had been put through the wringer at home, and I probably looked like that too. My hair was all over the place and I tried to straighten it and smooth it down a bit.

'Lend me your comb, will you?' I said.

He handed it over silently, and I struggled with my hair for a moment. Then he leant over and took it from me.

'You look all right to me,' he said. 'Leave it.'

It's not possible that a ride on a switchback could change a person, but that's what it seemed like. 'You look all right to me. Leave it.' Plain simple words, but songs to me, because they were natural. What anyone might have said.

'Come on,' he said then, taking my arm. 'Let's go and have supper somewhere.'

I thought we were going to one of those open air places, but it turned out he had other plans. This, too, was a different David from the one I had seen before. We went down to the pier and took the boat back to Westminster. Then we got into the car and he drove for a while until we came to a narrow street I'd never even been in before. In fact, I wasn't at all sure what part of London we were in. I left the googly-eyed doll in the car and Davie locked the doors.

He took my arm again and steered me across the road.

'What about this?' he said.

'Where are we?'

'I don't quite know. I've never been here before in my life. But what about it?'

I looked at him.

'Try anything once,' we both said together.

'Snap,' said Davie.

We went in.

IX

It was a small place with a low roof and red shades on
the lamps on each table. The table-cloths were red and
white checked material, quite simple. I had never been
inside a place like it before. We were taken to a corner
table and I glanced round as we sat down, trying not to
look at Davie, and trying at the same time to seem at
ease. It wasn't easy, as I had hardly ever been into
restaurants. I noticed the table-cloths weren't all that
clean, and that the soft lights threw shadows into the
corners and probably hid quite a lot of things they
would rather you didn't see. I wondered what Mother
would say. I could hear her voice: 'Well, I don't know,
but it's not very *clean*, dear, is it?' in that firm tone
she uses when she disapproves of anything.

A waiter in a cotton jacket brought us the menu,
one each, and we spent a lot of time choosing, because
we didn't know what the things were. But the waiter
was friendly.

That was the first thing that surprised me about
Davie. He ordered the food and spoke to the waiter as
if he did the same thing every day of his life. I had
said that I would have what he had, and so he took the
job seriously. We started with an omelette, and it was
very good. At least Mother would not have complained
on that score.

We didn't say much at first. I watched Davie while
he was talking to the waiter, and he looked stern and
old. His expression was very serious and I had to shake
myself to remember that he was eighteen, the same age
as I was. But then he always had looked old, even when
he was a small boy.

We talked a little while we were eating, mostly about the food, and it wasn't difficult. Of course we didn't have difficult things to say, but all the same, no one would have known that we had hardly ever actually spoken to each other before. But then, no one would believe what we *had* been doing anyhow.

When we were having coffee afterwards, I just couldn't help myself. Perhaps I ought not to have, but I simply had to ask him. I simply had to; to mention the subject we had never mentioned. It's impossible to start talking to someone suddenly like that, someone you've known for months in the way I knew him and he knew me, without saying something about it. I spent quite a long time trying to decide how to ask him.

'Davie . . . ?'

He looked up.

'Do you want to talk now?'

He picked up the coffee spoon and started drawing lines on the table-cloth with it, up and down the sides of the squares, slowly and carefully. It was quiet for rather a long time. Then he stopped the spoon and looked up again.

'Yes,' he said.

'You talk to waiters and people like that as if you were just like anyone else.' As soon as I had said it, I wished I hadn't because what I was actually saying was that he was peculiar, different, not like anyone else. Which, of course, was true.

But he didn't take it that way.

'Yes, I know,' he said. 'But I don't know them.'

'But you don't know anyone until you begin to talk to them.'

'I know, but waiters and bus conductors don't want

to know you, do they? They just want your fare, or your order. That's simple.'

I sat and said nothing. I thought I'd leave it to him. He started drawing squares again with the spoon, and then he suddenly put it back in his saucer.

'I've never talked to a girl before tonight,' he said. 'Not properly. Only things like "Yes, please", and "No, thank you" and "Excuse me" and things like that. It's true. I've never spoken to a girl, unless I've absolutely had to. Been forced to. And you can get away with very little, in fact. Nodding and shaking your head and so on.'

'The girls say you're unfriendly.'

'Do they talk about me?'

'Sometimes,' I said, remembering how I'd listened to their talk. 'But they think you don't like them. That you look down on them.'

'It's not true. Anything but true. I've never dared.'

He looked up and straight at me. For once I could actually see his eyes behind those glasses, and they were asking me to believe him.

'No,' I said. 'But there's no knowing, is there, if you never say anything.'

'They don't understand.'

There was a short silence while I thought how little I understood too.

'I don't really understand either,' I said, looking down into my coffee cup. 'Can you explain? What made you start talking just now? Why now and not before?'

'I don't really know,' he said slowly. 'It's been coming for some time.' Then he picked up the spoon again and started tapping his knuckle with it. 'I've never forgotten you,' he went on, not looking up. 'I've never forgotten you from that school.'

'All that time ago?'

' Yes,' he said. 'But it's not easy to forget either. I hated it. It may sound silly now, but I hated it as I've never hated anything since. I can't remember hating anything before, or anything I've hated so much since, but just that year in that school sticks in my head as the worst time I can remember.'

He stopped and gazed across the restaurant. The place was full and most people were talking quietly. Occasionally a burst of laughter came from a table on the other side of the room, where four people were having a meal together. Davie stared at them as if he had forgotten me, and then he went on speaking without looking at me.

'You were the only person that made it even bearable there. I really couldn't speak then. To anyone. I used to almost burst trying to. I can remember feeling as if my head would crack and my eyes pop out of my head.'

'Why were you like that?' I asked. 'Why? Do you know?'

Now he was talking so much, I hardly knew what to say. I wanted him to go on, but I didn't want him to get upset, and I didn't know whether raking all this up would upset him. But he didn't seem to mind. He looked down at his coffee cup and frowned.

'I don't really know,' he said. 'But now I'm older, I understand more about it. At that age you don't understand anything at all, and I certainly didn't understand what had happened to me. But now I can put two and two together and it begins to make sense.'

He poured out more coffee for both of us and fussed about with milk and sugar for a moment.

'My parents died years ago,' he went on. 'I don't even remember them, so it's nothing to do with that. At least, not directly. My grandmother brought me up. Nan, I always called her. I never realized she was so much older than other people's parents. Nor that she was often ill. She never said anything about it. But that's the worst of being young. You know so little and understand so little, you take everything for granted. And you think everyone will go on for ever. But she didn't. She died that year. The year I came to that school. They moved me to that area.'

He fell silent again, stirring the coffee for longer than any coffee ever needed stirring.

'I was living in a children's home. I hated that too, but I expect it was all right, really. It was just that it was so unlike Nan's place. No Nan, and no special meals for special occasions. No nothing that I remembered with Nan, just a lot of people I didn't know and the end of the world, as far as I was concerned. That's where I started not being able to speak at all.'

Suddenly he smiled.

'Mind you, I was never exactly a chatterbox. Nan always said I was a silent person. "Some little bird's taken your tongue again," she would say sometimes, and it was true that I used to sit and dream away sometimes and not say anything at all for hours on end. But Nan wasn't a great talker either. We just got on. Then she just wasn't there. That was the first time it happened that I found I couldn't speak, even if I wanted to. Some sort of shock, I suppose, which became a habit.'

'Did they do anything for it?'

'Oh, they tried to make me speak. But the more they

tried to make me say things, the worse it seemed to get. They thought I was just being cussed sometimes, and they got angry. But I wasn't. I could speak, but the words just wouldn't come out. They just wouldn't.'

His face screwed up as if he were remembering the effort of trying to speak. 'So the school got all mixed up with that, you see. I hated it. Hated it and hated everyone in it. Everyone. In fact I hardly even saw who they all were; all I knew was that I hated it. Then you started writing those notes. Remember?'

I just nodded and smiled.

'I remember the first one,' Davie said. 'Did you ever read that book?'

I shook my head.

'I thought not, even then. Anyhow, all that black hatred thinned out a bit then. Everything became possible instead of impossible.'

I tried to think what it would be like to be ten and know that everything was impossible, but I couldn't. At that age we take so much for granted, Davie had said. Yes. Family and friends and being able to talk.

'What about later on?' I said. 'How did you get on? At school and that sort of thing? After we moved away and all went to different schools?'

'It was all right. They left me alone, mostly. I liked the work. I still do. I like the work at Grant's. But I liked school work. You could sort of get yourself lost in it. I'd got some foster-parents by then, people I lived with, and then I sometimes spent holidays up in the north with some rather distant relatives. No one seemed to notice or mind that I hardly ever spoke to anyone. And I made quite sure I didn't have to speak to girls. Even now, every time anyone speaks to me, I can feel a knot tying itself up inside me. It gets tighter and tighter and I can't get the words out. It's far worse with girls. With some older women it's not so bad, people in shops and so on. But even in shops I avoid the girls. I suppose . . .'

He stopped fiddling with the spoon and his cup and held on to the edge of the table, looking straight at me again.

'. . . I suppose you could say that I can only speak to you because you're the only one who doesn't try to speak to me.'

'But I do. Or rather I did.'

'Yes, but you didn't directly. You didn't bounce out at me, expecting an answer. You didn't try to make me speak.'

Well, I would have done if I'd had the courage, I thought. I would have spoken to you, and if I'd been braver, I suppose I would never have started that game with the notes. Or would I? I remembered that awful Sunday, when I'd decided that I was the wrong person for Davie.

'What about work, though?'

'It's not so bad. They've got used to me now. They leave me alone. It's not difficult to talk about figures —accounts, balance sheets, costings and all that. They don't answer back. They aren't people. It's people I can't talk to or about. I suppose'—he hesitated, then went on—'I suppose, I'm afraid of people, and that's just what you're not supposed to be, if you're a man.'

'And the notes?' I said. 'Was it the notes that started you off?'

He smiled again. All this time he had been talking jerkily, often looking away, and it was hard to see his eyes through his glasses. He often hesitated, not quite stuttering, but talking a little uncertainly, as if he were choosing what he was saying very carefully. But having chosen he sounded quite sure of himself.

As I listened to him, I thought again, as I had that day I'd been to see him in that room of his, about how little I knew about him, or indeed how little I knew about anyone at all. It isn't only at ten years old that you take everything for granted. Here I was at eighteen, doing much the same. I lived with my family, and they seemed just like anyone else to me. But things had changed these last few months. It was almost as if my eyes had got sharper, and suddenly could see what they hadn't been able to see before. Before, I'd gone through a day, a week, a month, most of my life, I suppose, without ever really thinking about anyone else but myself. And now? What was different now? I couldn't have told anyone what it was, but it was as if I were more alive, less of a nobody, because here was someone I liked and had to think about in quite a different way from the way I thought about myself. And I was something different to him too. That made a difference.

Everyone had seemed more or less like me before, usually better and cleverer. Everyone seemed to have parents and brothers and sisters and homes, bigger or smaller, poorer or richer. Not everyone, of course. Some didn't. We all knew that. But now I actually knew Davie, it was more than just knowing one of those people who were different and hadn't got families in the same way. It was like seeing a great hole in front of you—a great empty hole. And somehow, almost without knowing I had done it, I had become useful to someone. It was me he wanted to talk to. Me.

And those notes. It had been a childish game, and I
had known it. A childish game, which was why I hadn't
wanted anyone to know, why I had kept it secret from
everyone, because I had known it was childish and
although I had said to myself I didn't want anyone to
laugh at Davie, poor Daftie Davie, who didn't speak,
in fact I knew it was because I hadn't wanted anyone
to laugh at *me*, for being childish too. But it was no
game for Davie. It was a kind of lifeline for him, the
only way he could make himself like everyone else.

He was talking more easily now.

'I used to see you standing by that tree every day,'
he said. 'Every day as I drove home. At first, I couldn't
think why you looked so familiar. But when it got
warmer and you often had nothing on your head, it
was your hair that made me remember. Your red hair.
I kept thinking, where have I seen someone with red
hair like that before? After two or three times, I remembered, and then it suddenly all came back to me,
that note business at school. I thought about it a lot,
but it was weeks before I decided to start again. I'd
dismissed the idea at first . . . as stupid. Childish.
Then I knew I wouldn't dare. Then I began making
up conversations with you in my head. Then one day
I thought I'd see if you remembered me. Crazy, I
know.'

'What made you actually do it?'

'I don't know. A sort of desperation, I think. Or I'd
burst. Like trying to talk. I put that first note in the
tree and at first I thought you'd never see it. Then I
began to hope and pray you wouldn't. Then I had sort
of nightmares of what would happen if you did and
told them all at work. I nearly went and took it out

again, but then you found it. I had a pretty bad few days then, wondering what you'd do. Daftie Davie.'

He smiled when he said the name.

'So you haven't forgotten that then?' I said.

'It's not the sort of thing you ever forget,' he said shortly.

We went on talking for a long time. We talked about all kinds of things, not just ourselves and work. We went on until I suddenly noticed that there were no more customers left except us two, and the waiter was hovering about looking in our direction.

'Davie,' I said, 'what's the time?'

He looked at his watch.

'It's after midnight!'

We sat staring at each other, saying nothing, then I started getting up.

'Mother'll have a fit!'

We held hands as we walked towards the car, and Davie was quite silent all the way back.

'See you tomorrow,' was all he said just before he shut the car door. The warm atmosphere of the restaurant had gone and there was something closed about his face again too. But I was happy, almost excited.

Mother hadn't actually had a fit, but she was waiting up for me, and she was very angry, more angry than I have ever seen her before in my life. She thought I'd been in a car crash or something like that, or much worse things, and they all poured out of her as she stood there in the hall, her dressing-gown wrapped round her, her hair ruffled and her face red and flushed. She went on and on, though I think she was angry with me out of relief at seeing me back safe and sound more than anything else. I didn't say anything, for once, and let her go on until she had no breath left for more. Then I drew a deep breath. Never have I felt so sure of myself and so unafraid of her. Almost as if we were the same age.

'Mother,' I said, as carefully and coolly as possible, though I was certainly not feeling cool, standing there in the hall, clutching that silly doll. 'Don't go on so any more. Please. Please, Mother. It's all right. I haven't done anything wrong. I promise you. Nothing wrong at all. It just got terribly late, that's all, and we never noticed the time. We weren't doing anything to be ashamed of, or that you need worry about. We were only talking. That's all.'

She calmed down. She must have believed me, I think. And I was telling the truth. But she couldn't possibly have known what I meant when I said that 'we were only talking'.

I slept and slept, and woke up very late the next morning. It was just as well I still had some holiday left. I lay in bed thinking. It may sound as if that was the end of this story, but of course it wasn't. It was hardly the beginning.

X

It was only the beginning. I soon found that out. We both went back to work again and, for a week or two, Davie just gave me a lift home at the end of the day, and that was all I saw of him. He talked more, of course, but quite often he would say nothing all the way, just as before.

'I know you don't mind,' he said once. 'You're the only person I can talk to. And you're the only person who'll put up with me when I don't talk, too.'

I said nothing, but inside I wondered what would happen. At work there was a lot to do, more than usual. There always is a lot to do after the holidays, as there were orders waiting to be filled and new girls, too, who had to be helped. This meant that there was a lot of overtime to be done, so I often missed my ride home.

The girls were curious. They asked about Davie, sometimes indirectly, but sometimes straight out.

'How did you get to know him?' one asked me one day, as we were changing to go home, very late again.

'What's he like?' said another, before I'd had time to think of an answer to the first one.

'Do you just say nothing to each other all the time?' another girl asked. All the others in the cloakroom laughed.

I didn't laugh with them. As just saying nothing to each other was exactly what we did do quite often, it was hardly funny to me. I couldn't possibly explain either, not without telling them everything, and I didn't want to do that. I don't think I would even have been able to explain and I knew Davie would have hated it if he'd known I was talking about him to the other girls. So I just said nothing and told them nothing. They thought I was standoffish, I know, and some of them ignored me after that. They didn't like me for it, and added to the fact that Davie worked in the office, that made it all very difficult. I think they thought I was like Davie and looked down on them. Which wasn't true, of course, just as it wasn't true of Davie. How could they know that I had envied them before, with their free and easy ways, their good looks and their friends, everything I hadn't got.

I didn't envy them now, but it wasn't pleasant to find they didn't like me. And I didn't tell Davie either. Once when we had been to the cinema together one rainy evening, we stopped at a coffee bar afterwards, and I asked him what he usually did in the evenings.

'Work usually,' he said. 'I've got a lot more exams to get through. Or I read, or listen to the wireless . . .'

He stopped suddenly and looked up at me.

'Are you getting sick of me?' he said quickly.

'Of course not,' I said quickly back. 'But it seems a lonely life. In that room. All by yourself. It's not a very . . .'

I couldn't go on. Every time I thought of that bare room, I remembered that awful Sunday. I'd never mentioned it again, and neither had Davie.

'It's not very what?' he said.

'Well, it's a bit . . . a bit . . .'

I couldn't go on.

'I know,' he said. 'I know, but it's the only place I feel really O.K. in, you see. I've got used to it. It's **mine**. It's . . .'

His voice tailed off and I saw his fists clench.

'Why was it so awful when I came round that day?' I said, the words rushing out of my mouth.

He looked up, and there was that same look in his eyes again, asking me to believe him, almost pleading.

'Because I couldn't speak,' he said. 'I just could not and it's never been so bad as when you were there. Never.' He stopped for a moment, and then went on. 'You know, I have wondered sometimes whether I'm queer in the head, and when you came that day, for a moment I thought I wasn't going to be able to say anything at all. It was a shock to see you there, and every sensible thing went straight out of my head. I wanted to sing and dance and say come in, and give you tea and talk and talk and talk and talk. God knows, I'd often thought about it. Over and over again, I'd imagined you there, sitting in that very chair, and we were talking just like anyone else. But it was all quite different when you actually were there. All I could do was to say nothing at all, and all I wanted to do was to cry out aloud for help. You left just in time. So you see, I'm not to be trusted. Yet.'

I knew what he meant by 'yet'. He still dropped me outside the house every evening, but he always refused to come in. I had asked him once or twice, but he had just shaken his head.

'I couldn't,' he said. 'I'd get tied up in knots. I can't face it. It'd wreck everything. Can't you see that? What would your parents think?'

I didn't know. What would Mother and Dad think? And Bruce? I went cold at the thought of what Bruce might do without meaning any harm. He'd be awful and I could just see him rolling round the place, laughing in that explosive way he has. Mother had been asking questions too, the kind of questions which are hard to answer truthfully, if you don't tell the whole truth.

'Why don't you bring him in one day, Tina,' she said.

'He has to get on home.'

'Where does he live, then?'

'Oh, not far away. But he's always in a hurry.'

'In a hurry to get away from us, I suppose.'

'No, he's not like that.'

'What's his family like, then?'

'He hasn't got much family. Not here, anyhow.'

'Perhaps he thinks we're not good enough for him and his likes,' said Mother, huffily, cross because I was giving her evasive answers.

'Oh, no, he's not like that at all,' I protested. 'He's just shy, that's all. He'll come one day, I expect.'

'Hmm,' said Mother. 'We'll believe that when we see him.'

He did come one day in the end. It wasn't until some time later, but he came. It was simple, and I can't think why I hadn't thought of it before. I wrote a note.

Look in the tree.

I gave the note to one of the girls in the office, in an envelope, all stuck up with *Mr Rawlins* written on the outside. I asked her to put it on his desk and gave no explanation.

The other note I wrote on a card. I wrote it carefully, doing the lettering as they do on invitation cards, loopy and formal.

Mr and Mrs George Carter, and their daughter

*Christina, request the pleasure of Mr David Rawlins'
company for lunch on Sunday at 1 o'clock.*

I looked at it. It didn't look very professional, and
one of the lines sloped downwards. It wouldn't do. So
I sneaked into one of the offices during the lunch hour
and typed it out, with one finger, on to another card.
It looked very cold and pompous, like an invitation to
Buckingham Palace, or to an official dinner. I remembered the wording from one Dad had had sent to him
when he got his medal. Only that was just for him and
Mother, and that had been printed.

I still hadn't told Mother. In fact, I hadn't even
asked her if Davie could come on Sunday. It was just
like balancing on a tight-rope, or something like that.
But if I asked her first and then Davie refused, there
would be more remarks like 'not good enough for us,
I suppose'. If I asked Davie first, and he accepted, and
then she refused, what would I do then? Oh, well, I'd
have to face that one when I came to it, I thought. I
was really getting quite reckless. For me.

I rolled the card up and stuck it into the hole in the
tree, leaving a very small bit showing. All that day, I
lurked about in the grounds whenever I could get a
chance to get out, and looked across the road to see if
Davie were there. That was something I had never
done before. And of course, he wasn't there. In the
evening, I didn't know if the card was still there or not
and I said nothing at all in the car on the way home.

The next day I couldn't even wait until the lunch
hour. I went diving across the road in my overall, my
hair all tied up in a cloth, and I didn't even bother to
look round to see if anyone were watching. When I
thought about how cautious I had been before, always

making sure there was no one about before even glancing up at the tree, and even then slipping the note out as if I were a thief or a shop-lifter, I laughed at myself. What did it matter if anyone saw, anyhow?

There were a few people walking about on the pavement, but they didn't even glance at me. I walked straight up to the tree, stood on tiptoe and looked.

There was a note there. A card. For a moment, I thought it was the one I had put there, but it wasn't. It was different and had curved corners. There it was, sticking out of the bark. I pulled it out and nearly got run over as I crossed the road back to work. A lorry driver swore loudly at me through the cab window, but I never even turned back to look.

Mr David Rawlins has much pleasure in accepting your kind invitation for Sunday at 1 o'clock.

That was all. Typed, even more neatly than mine had been. I wondered if he had done it himself, or whether he had asked one of the girls to do it. Himself, I expect. He was coming.

I stuffed the card into my overall pocket and went on into the canteen. It was very noisy in there, but I just fetched my lunch and ate it and went back to the machine room without looking or speaking to anyone, my thoughts racing round and round in my head. My idea had worked. Perhaps the stiff words had made it seem as if we weren't people, not real people. The formal invitation wasn't like someone speaking to him. It had worked. Or perhaps it had just made it easier for him to give in and have a try.

But that was only the beginning too. Now I had to ask Mother. I was working late that night, so the others had all had tea when I got in. Mother was just wiping

down the draining-board. She got my plate out of the
oven and put it down in front of me.

'Mother,' I said, picking up my knife and fork and
glaring down at the food without saying anything. 'Can
David come to Sunday dinner?'

Mother had sat down at the table again and was
pouring out tea for me and another cup for herself.

'Not this Sunday, dear, no,' she said, quite casually.
'It's not enough notice. Next Sunday will give me more
time to get the place straight.'

That was just like Mother. I stuffed a piece of bacon
into my mouth and chewed furiously. The house is
always fit for a king to come into, at any time of the
day or night. But if anyone does come, she cleans and
polishes and dusts until it's dangerous to walk anywhere and the rugs fly about in all directions if you so
much as touch them. I swallowed the bacon, which
tasted like blotting-paper.

'Please, Mother,' I said. 'It's . . . it's terribly important.'

She must have heard something in my voice this
time, for she looked up sharply and put her cup down
in the saucer.

'And why, may I ask, is it so terribly important all
of a sudden?'

'Because . . .'

So I told her. It seemed the right moment. Dad was
in the other room and Bruce had gone out after tea.
I told her everything in the end. About how I'd known
him at the other school. About how strange he'd been.
I even told her about the notes and the tree. I hardly
dared look at her, in case she laughed when I told her
about that, and I stared and stared down into the dregs

in my cup, as if it were dreadfully important that I should count every one of the tea-leaves there. But she didn't laugh.

Then I told her why I had been so late the night we'd been to Battersea.

'He wouldn't come here, you see,' I said. 'He said he just couldn't and I couldn't tell you why. But now he says he will, or rather, he says he has much pleasure in accepting our kind invitation.'

I giggled a bit when I said that, a croaky sound, and then I stopped talking.

Mother said nothing for quite a long time. I couldn't fathom what she was thinking by looking at her face. There was no expression on it at all. Then she took the cosy off the teapot and poured herself out another cup of tea. It must have been at least her fourth.

'Poor boy,' she said. 'What a thing, now. What a time he must have had, to be like that. Poor thing.'

I could have hugged her. Instead, I said:

'Mother, you'll have to tell Dad, I know, but please Mother, *please* don't let on that you know. That I've told you all this. Please pretend you know nothing. If he says nothing . . . if he can't say anything . . . please don't take any notice. Tell Dad not to, too, won't you . . .'

I must have sounded very worried, because she leant over the table suddenly and stroked my cheek, a thing she hasn't done for years and years, since I was very small. I suddenly felt weepy, but managed to be sensible.

'There, love,' she said. 'What do you think we are then? We're not that bad. We'll do what we can. And

your Dad's a good man, you know that. He wouldn't
hurt a fly. He'll understand.'

'And Bruce?' I said. 'Will you speak to him? You
mustn't tell him *anything*, please.'

'I'll deal with young Bruce, never you mind,' said
Mother, in her you-just-keep-quiet-and-listen-to-me
tone of voice. 'Don't you worry your head about him.'

But, of course, I did worry, and not just about Bruce.

XI

Davie took me home twice after that, on the Wednesday and the Thursday, and he said nothing about it. I knew Mother had been flying round the house, determined that everything should be just so, and Bruce had been muttering and Dad saying nothing at all, but just looking at me all the time. But somehow I thought that if I brought the subject up, Davie might change his mind, just as on the day I'd gone to see him in his room. So I managed to say nothing. Then on the Friday, just before I got out of the car, he put his hand on my arm and said: 'See you Sunday.'

I nodded and smiled and got out. I couldn't have said anything even if I had tried.

I kept out of Mother's way on Sunday and no one said anything. At ten to one, I heard Davie's car coming down the road. I suppose I had been listening all the time. I went out and took him into the house. Mother came out of the kitchen and I introduced him to her and to Dad.

'This is David.'

Dad shook hands with him and Mother just beamed.

'I must go and dish up the dinner,' she said. 'I won't be long. You come and help, will you, Tina?'

I looked at Dad and then at Davie. Davie looked anxious. Then Dad said: 'I've got some birds nesting in the garden. Optimists they are, at this time of year. But still, you never know. Come and have a look, David, while the women are busy.'

They disappeared into our little garden, Dad plodding out through the garden door and down the garden path, without looking behind him. Mother and I went into the kitchen and I could see David following Dad, and then they stopped by the rose-bush which Dad has been nursing along for such a time. Dad was pointing at the nesting-box he'd nailed on to the post and he was shaking his head. I knew what he was telling Davie—that he'd put the nesting-box there so that the birds would think the bush was a tree and would perhaps come and nest in it. But they hadn't. Sometimes they had looked it over, like prospective tenants, but this was the first time any bird had settled there—somewhat late too. I could almost hear Dad's little joke, which we had all heard a hundred times before. 'Of course, they're so fussy nowadays, young marrieds. Not like in my day.'

Just as Dad leant forward to peer into the box, a bird suddenly flew out of the hole and darted away over into the next-door garden. Both Dad and Davie took a step backwards in surprise, and then they both looked at each other and laughed. Then Davie said something to Dad. I saw his lips moving. Then Dad opened the lid of the nesting-box and they both leant over and looked inside like a couple of naughty kids. I could feel myself smiling.

Mother poked me in the back.

'Come on,' she said. 'Gawping at them won't get the dinner on the table. Leave them be. They'll be all right.'

She was right, of course. Everything turned out all right. There was a lot of talking over the meal, and whenever Davie got stuck, Mother asked Dad something, or Dad launched into one of his stories. I must say I never thought I would be glad to hear one of his stories again, as Bruce and I are always complaining that he tells them over and over again until everyone is sick to death of them. But today they seemed new and we all smiled when Davie smiled, as if we had never in our lives heard that one before.

Davie seemed happy, but it was hard to tell what he was thinking. He was polite and he talked as much as he usually does to me. He never once looked at me directly. Mother had of course cooked a marvellous dinner, and we were using the best china, but I hardly tasted the food. I ate it, that's all.

Bruce didn't say a word. He just sat there, as if butter wouldn't melt in his mouth, and when Davie actually asked him a question about what he was going to do when he left school, he suddenly blushed and turned awkward, so Dad had to fill in for him. I wondered what on earth Mother had said to him, because he usually chattered on through meals and it was hard for anyone else to get a word in edgeways. But not today. Nothing was the same today.

After dinner, Davie and Dad went into the other room and Mother and I cleared away.

Mother smiled and chaffed me.

'I thought you said he didn't talk,' she said. 'Bruce was the one who was struck dumb. I think it was those spectacles that impressed him most. Wouldn't be surprised if he's not asking for a pair for himself next.'

Davie thanked Mother and Dad soon after and I walked out to the car with him.

'Come for a run round,' he said.

'All right, I'll just get my coat.'

'No, don't. It's not cold. I'll bring you back here.'

I got in and we drove round for a while, not saying

anything. Then Davie stopped the car in a lay-by and turned to look at me.

'It was all right, wasn't it?' I said.

He nodded.

'It's been the worst week I can remember,' he said. 'Worse than that week when I sat around wondering whether you would see that note, and then wondering what you would do if you did.'

'Why was this week so awful?'

'Well, it was almost the same as before. Like turning the clock back. As soon as I had put that card in the tree, I wished I hadn't. And then I hadn't the nerve to go and take it away, and yet I knew if I left it there, I'd have to come today.'

'But it wasn't that bad was it? Mother and Dad were pleased to see you. They liked you. I could tell that.'

'Well it's easy to say that now. I can't think what I was in such a state about now. Stupid, isn't it? I know it's stupid. I have always known, but it takes someone else to show you what to do about it.'

'Oh, well,' I said. 'Try anything once seems to be quite a good motto, doesn't it? Like the switchback.'

He grinned. 'Come on,' he said. 'I'll take you back now. It's been a long day.'

When we got back, he got out and opened the door on my side of the car.

I got out. As we were standing there, the car door between us, he suddenly leant over the door and kissed me gently on the cheek.

'Thanks,' he said. 'See you tomorrow.'

I went into the house, where everything was much the same as usual. Bruce nodded at me in quite a friendly way. Dad opened his eyes, grunted and then closed them again. Mother just looked up from the television, smiled and then turned back to the programme. None of them even noticed that for me everything was completely different, anything but the same as usual.

There is only one small bit of this story left. On the Monday after that Sunday, a very odd thing happened. At first, I didn't notice anything. I went to work in the morning, half-awake as usual, but as I was walking down the side of the main building, I began to feel very uneasy. I couldn't think why. It was a fine autumn morning, the sky blue and clear and the sun out already. But something kept niggling at me, as if I had forgotten something, or left my bag on the bus, or come to the wrong place. I couldn't think what it was. I stopped so suddenly that a girl coming behind me ran straight into me.

'Hey, look what you're doing, can't you.'

I said I was sorry and just stood there, trying to think what was wrong. Girls and men streamed past me, but I scarcely noticed them. I looked back the way I had come and then I saw at once what it was.

The tree had gone.

It just wasn't there any longer. Someone had been there over the weekend and cut it down. All that was to be seen which showed that there had ever been anything there at all was a rough heap of mud and gravel on the pavement.

At first I thought I must be dreaming. Then I realized I wasn't, and that it was Monday morning, and the tree was gone. I had to tell Davie. Without thinking, I ran back the way I had come, against the stream of people, and went in through the main door, the quickest way to the offices. I met Davie in the corridor and stopped in front of him, quite out of breath by now.

For a moment a look of fright appeared in his eyes and I saw him go pale. Then I burst out with it.

'Davie, look! Have you seen?'

I held on to his arm and pointed through the glass doors.

'Look. The tree. Our tree. They've cut it down! It's gone. I've only just noticed.'

At first he looked startled. I think that was the last thing he had expected me to say. Then he looked at me again and back across at where the tree had once stood.

'Oh, well,' he said slowly. 'It's a pity. I liked that old tree. But we don't need it any longer.'